Bolan charged through the door to face the gunners

A pair of hardmen glanced up from their conversations, then froze for an instant as the Executioner lobbed two grenades and ducked out of sight.

Returning to the scene of carnage with the Uzi up and ready, he emptied the magazine, the parabellum shockers finishing a job that shrapnel had begun.

Reloading on the move, Bolan reached inside his satchel for a smoke grenade and rushed the other dining room. He tossed the grenade across the room and raked the ceiling with a burst that shattered the ornate light fixtures. One of the diners was braced to fire an automatic, and the warrior let him have one free shot before dropping him in his tracks. The others were stretched prone or scrambling toward the street, and Bolan let them go.

His point was made.

The Executioner was in town, and Medellín would never be the same.

MACK BOLAN.

The Executioner

DON PENDLETON'S
THE EXECUTIONER®
FEATURING MACK BOLAN®

MESSAGE TO MEDELLÍN

A GOLD EAGLE BOOK FROM
WORLDWIDE.

TORONTO · NEW YORK · LONDON · PARIS
AMSTERDAM · STOCKHOLM · HAMBURG
ATHENS · MILAN · TOKYO · SYDNEY

First edition July 1991

ISBN 0-373-61151-X

Special thanks and acknowledgment to
Mike Newton for his contribution to this work.

MESSAGE TO MEDELLÍN

Only he can understand what a farm is, what a country is, who shall have sacrificed part of himself to his farm or his country.

—Saint-Exupery

Without duty, life is soft and boneless. It cannot hold itself together.

—Joseph Joubert

Sometimes, the exercise of duty demands a sacrifice. And sometimes, with a bit of luck, you have a chance to sacrifice your enemies.

—Mack Bolan

To the law-abiding people of Colombia

1

"If we're not in time," Hermann "Gadgets" Schwarz said, "I swear to God I'll kick somebody's ass at the DEA."

"Relax." Behind the wheel Pol Blancanales kept his eyes peeled for a sign announcing the marina and their exit from the traffic swarming Miami's Bay Shore Drive. "We're lucky we even got the call."

"I guess."

"You *know*. The way we sidestepped DEA on this, I'm half surprised they even passed the word to Stony Man."

"No choice," Leo Turrin said from the backseat. "Hal had the local office covered going in."

"A mole?"

"Let's say a friend in need."

"Who phoned it in?"

"A girlfriend. Sheila Something. She was playing cagey, but they put an automatic trace on all their breather calls at DEA."

"We're firm on Constantine?"

"Beyond a shadow. He's been working with Costanza for the past five years at least. Incorporating fronts, defending runners now and then. He runs a decent laundry on the side. Your dirty money comes out spick-and-span, no starch."

"I would've pegged a guy like that to stick it out," Schwarz said.

"He tried. The trouble is, he's built up quite a file at Justice, not to mention Treasury and Stony Man Farm. Somebody tipped him off that fighting the Ortega extradition might present some problems with the alphabet—like the ABA, the IRS, the FBI, the DEA...."

"I wish I could've seen the bastard's face," Schwarz said.

"It's coming up," Blancanales replied, signaling the turn off Bay Shore Drive. In front of them the harbor bristled with masts and spars. "We're looking for a Chris Craft forty-footer, the *Hung Jury*."

"Lawyer humor," Turrin groused. "How many pushers do you think it takes to get yourself a berth at the marina?"

"One ought to do it, if his name's Costanza."

Blancanales parked their unmarked four-door near the water, and the team spent a moment double-checking side arms, locking doors behind them as they left the car.

"He'll want to see a warrant," Turrin said.

"So we can reason with him," Blancanales answered. "I've got four days' worth of unresolved hostility I'd love to spread around."

It had been four days since they'd lost Carl Lyons on a milk run to the home of an informant, one Maria Teresina, four days during which they'd discovered that their "informant" was a principal in the Costanza drug cartel. Her enemies had dubbed the lady La Araña—the spider—after her facility for snaring and dispatching human prey.

Four days could be a lifetime, and with every passing hour Schwarz and Blancanales knew their odds of finding Lyons safe and sound were dwindling. The only point in keeping him alive this long would be interrogation or a trade, and there had been no ransom overtures so far. If Lyons was being grilled by the Colombians for information, then survival might not be a blessing, after all.

Leo Turrin seemed to read Politician's morbid thoughts. "We'll get him back," the man from Justice said. "I've got a feeling."

"That's the problem. So do I."

Each of them had seen the pitiful remains of syndicate interrogation victims in the past. Some of the old-line mafiosi used to call them "turkeys" after they were carved and reassembled with a surgeon's skill. It was a twisted kind of artform, sculpting human flesh and dragging out the misery until the only conscious thought remaining was a prayer for death.

If the Colombians had nicknames for their victims, Blancanales hadn't heard them yet. No matter. If you'd seen one turkey, you'd seen them all.

"We've got a winner, boys and girls," Turrin said.

The Chris Craft was a beauty, freshly painted white and baby blue, with hardware polished to a mirror shine. Her name was stenciled on the bow and the stern in gold metallic paint.

"Some tub," Schwarz muttered, and he spit into the water at their feet.

"You want to kill the fish?" Blancanales cracked.

"I'd rather shoot a weasel, if I've got a choice."

"He's out of season," Turrin said. "Until he tells us where to find the lady, anyway."

Politician felt a nervous itching in his palms. He knew they were lucky, catching Alexander Constantine before he sailed for the Bahamas and reached the first of several numbered bank accounts that waited from him, safely out of reach of the IRS. Another hour and their pigeon could have been in Nassau, soaking up the sun.

"If we're going in," Schwarz said, "let's get it done."

They moved past other yachts, some smaller than the Chris Craft, others slightly larger. Two or three had people out on deck, the women wearing next to nothing, lean and bronze. Politician caught a tall blonde watching from the shaded cabin of a thirty-footer, next in line. It cost him something to return her sparkling smile.

"A friend of yours?" Turrin asked.

"Don't I wish."

"She's half your age."

"The better half," Schwarz added, grinning for the first time in the past four days.

"You think so?" Blancanales joked. "Some days on the road I've got the ladies beating down my door."

"Hell, yes. They all want out."

There was no sign of life on board the Chris Craft, which was tied off fore and aft, the gangplank down.

"You figure he's expecting company?" Schwarz asked.

"Whatever," Blancanales replied. "He's got some now."

"Go easy," Turrin cautioned. "If he's on the run, chances are he's packing."

"So am I," Politician answered grimly.

He had one hand tucked inside his nylon jacket, covering the butt of his Beretta automatic as he started up the ramp.

IT HAD BEEN a long four days, thought Leo Turrin, bringing up the rear. He'd caught the red-eye down from Wonderland the same night Lyons disappeared, for all the good it had done. Ostensibly his job was limited to running interference with the local cops and the DEA for Able Team, preserving any vestige of the unit's cover that survived. But killing time behind a desk had never been Leo's style. In fact, he'd been dogging Schwarz and Blancanales as they made their rounds, corralling snitches, pressing every button they could find.

And all in vain.

Four wasted days, with Lyons in the wind and La Araña spinning brand-new webs in some dark corner of the city, safely tucked away and out of sight. Meanwhile, in Panama and Medellín, the world had simply come unglued.

Invasion.

The man from Justice could never have predicted the dramatic change of course in U.S. policy toward Panama— Hector Caseros stripped of power, tanks and airborne troops surrounding the place he'd chosen for sanctuary.

And somewhere in the middle of it all, the men of Phoenix Force had somehow managed to survive. Again.

In Medellín the situation was just as serious. A group of U.S. journalists had been mowed down by so-called revolutionaries in a bar, and the latest minister of justice had damn near been shredded by a bomb while speaking to an audience of several hundred on a public street. Mack Bolan and Jack Grimaldi were doing everything they could to undermine the narcobarons and divert their energies toward fratricidal warfare. And in retaliation, innocent people had died.

The Stony Man warriors had gone into the mission with a ten-day deadline and Leo Turrin couldn't swear that they'd gained an inch of ground, so far. The extradition, of Esteban Ortega, Luis Costanza's right-hand man, should count for something, granted, but experience had shown that even prime lieutenants were expendable.

The trade went on, in spite of ambushed dealers and intercepted shipments. Given time, Costanza's second-string competitors would find a way to take advantage of the shooting war, make fortunes while the ranking wheels were jarred off the track.

Still, Turrin couldn't bring himself to believe that it had been a waste. You played the cards as they were dealt and raised the ante where you could. Beyond that, it was up to fate or providence, or something he couldn't define.

He half expected to be challenged once they reached the deck, aware that every step they took was audible below. But as they made a circuit of the cabin, glancing in through tinted windows, working back around to the companionway, there was still nothing.

"You think he made a shopping run or something?" Gadgets asked.

Politician frowned. "We won't know until we check it out."

They stood in the companionway, their shadows merging to create the likeness of a gross, three-headed monster on the aft bulkhead.

"Fifty-fifty he went out for something he forgot," Schwarz suggested.

"Must be the second fifty I don't like."

"You want to stand around out here and wait, or what?"

"Screw that. I'm going in."

With the Beretta in his right hand, Blancanales used his left to knock. The door was off its latch, and Turrin drew his own .357 Magnum as it swung away, a wedge of darkness opening in front of them.

"Well, shit," the Justice man muttered.

"Hello?" Politician waited, then tried again. *"Hello?"*

"Nobody home," Schwarz said.

A whiff of something rank reached their nostrils simultaneously, and Turrin wrinkled his nose. "You want to bet?"

"God *damn* it!" Blancanales hit the open doorway in a rush, the others following with guns in hand. A touch of claustrophobia crowded in on them, despite the vessel's size and luxury. The galley was on their right, with dining on the left. Ahead of them loomed the cabins, closed and silent.

Pol found the one they wanted, just by following his nose. It was the kind of stench that was never quite forgotten— stale urine mixed with fecal matter when the sphincter muscle gave out and bowels unloaded in the last extreme.

The smell of violent death.

It was enough for Turrin, smelling it, to know what he would find beyond the door. He didn't have to look—the details hardly mattered—but he forced himself. He hadn't come this far to flinch and turn away.

Observing was the least he could do.

In front of him Pol shifted to his left and let Schwarz pass. As Gadgets moved to starboard, Turrin had his first and only glimpse of Alexander Constantine, Miami's hottest criminal attorney, in the flesh ... or what was left of it.

"Costanza's people?" Blancanales wondered out loud.

"Had to be," Turrin agreed.

"They found out he was running, and it didn't wash," Gadgets said.

"One thing's for sure," Pol added. "He won't be singing now."

"If he does," Gadgets said, "I'll go halfsies with you on the movie rights."

IT WAS A NECKTIE JOB, a signature technique perfected by Colombians for sending cowards, traitors and suspected stoolies on to their reward. In spite of secondhand descriptions and the crime-scene photos passed around at Stony Man, it was the first time Schwarz had seen the butchery, up close and personal.

For starters, Constantine had been subdued somehow. Fresh bruises on his cheek and forehead told the story of a beating. On the floor, beside his chair, there was a blood-stained handkerchief that might have served the killers as a temporary gag.

When they were finished with their work, of course, the gag would be unnecessary.

The forensics team could try to find the roll of duct tape, if they wanted to, but Gadgets thought the killers would have carried it away. There was no point in checking out the tape they left behind for fingerprints, but someone would undoubtedly be ordered to perform the tests, regardless. It was SOP with Homicide, and there were rituals to be observed.

The tape was gray and it had been wrapped around the lawyer's wrists and calves, a final loop around his chest to guarantee he couldn't escape the ornate captain's chair.

Aside from crusty scabs around one nostril, all the blood had come from a horrendous throat wound. It was almost ear-to-ear, a deep half-moon incision carved beneath the lawyer's chin, bisecting the carotid artery and jugular on either side. His short-sleeved shirt had been a powder yellow once upon a time, but it was deepest crimson now with rusty patches where the spill was nearly dry.

The "necktie" part of it relied on someone's grim imagination, but Schwarz couldn't fault the overall analogy. It must have been a trick, he thought, to reach inside the gaping wound with Constantine alive and thrashing, snare his tongue and sever the connective tissue holding it in place, then drag the whole thing out and drape it onto his chest.

No simple task, but they had pulled it off.

Damn right.

"If we could find out how they knew he was skipping," Blancanales said, "at least we'd have a lead."

"The girlfriend knew," Schwarz suggested.

"No good. If she was talking to Costanza, why call and tip the DEA?"

"So," Schwarz said. "Constantine told someone else he was leaving...or they had him wired."

"You think?"

"I wouldn't rule it out."

Politician scratched his head. "Okay. For what it's worth, we'll have forensics tear the boat apart. The penthouse, too. There might be something we can use."

"Too long," Gadgets said. "We're working on day five."

"I know what goddamn day it is, all right?" Blancanales snapped. "If you've got something else—"

"The girlfriend," Schwarz insisted again. "Sheila Something."

"What about her?"

"Worth a drive-by, anyway. She knew Constantine was splitting. We could see what else she knows."

On deck the salt air helped to cut the smell of death. Schwarz stashed the Browning automatic in its jackass rig and felt Politician's eyes upon him as he turned. "Day five, you know? I think I'm losing it."

Schwarz took the proffered hand, pumped it once and let it go. "I'll be the judge of that."

"You'll let me have a swift kick if I start to slide?"

"My pleasure. Size thirteen."

"Okay. What say we call this sucker in and take a ride?"

"I thought you'd never ask."

Below them, waiting on the dock, the man from Justice raised his voice. "You lovebirds want to shake a leg?"

"Shake this, why don't you?" Blancanales cracked.

"I'd be glad to, if I had a pair of tweezers and a magnifying glass."

Schwarz joined their banter, glad to put the yacht behind him, but he knew they were whistling past the graveyard. Alexander Constantine, in death, had given them a glimpse of what they might discover if and when they tracked down Carl Lyons. The same fate—or a variation on the theme— might lie in store for each and every one of them before Miami gave up her secrets.

Day five, and there was only one thing in the world they could count on.

They were quickly running out of time.

2

Mack Bolan gauged the leap at twelve feet, maximum, an easy hop from one roof to another, with an alley in between. No sweat... except that any slip from this point on would send him plunging to the littered pavement below.

The least he could count on in a drop like that was broken legs and gross internal damage, possibly a shattered spine. If he got turned around somehow and hit head-first... Well, either way, it was a lousy way to start the day in Medellín.

Twelve feet looked farther all the time.

Across the alley Bolan's target was a roof identical in all respects to the one he already occupied. Antennae sprouted here and there like spindly saplings stripped of leaves in winter, several of them twisted out of shape or snapped off at the roots. He faced a faded, peeling door that granted access to the floors below.

In theory there was no one home. The tenement had been condemned for faulty wiring, sanitary violations and the like—a testimony to its sad condition in a city where the poor made homes of cardboard packing crates and sheets of rusty tin. Somewhere along the line a landlord had acquired official enemies or seen a chance to profit from eviction of his tenants, and the building had been vacant now for several months.

Except for those who occupied the middle floor.

It was a decent compromise: too far above the street for most pedestrians to notice indications of activity, not high enough for errant shafts of light to stand out like a beacon in the darkest night. The fourth-floor windows had been hung with heavy draperies or painted over on the inside of the glass to frustrate prying eyes. The squatters came and went in darkness, using exits at the side and rear that they were always careful to secure with bolts and heavy bars.

It stood to reason that the landlord was involved, perhaps for money, since a cursory inspection of the building would have blown the squatters' game. For all that Bolan knew the tenement was paying more today than it had ever paid when it was filled with honest families, employed sporadically at hard-scratch jobs in Medellín.

One lesson he'd learned from the beginning of his private war: it was a sucker bet to underestimate the profit margin of corruption in society.

For all that, the illicit tenants could afford to pay the going price for silence and security. They worked no steady trade, but money came their way from ransom drops and daylight robberies, extortion bids against the rich and famous, seasonal donations from the Cuban treasury, and, on the side, selling themselves as hired assassins to the leaders of the Medellín cartel.

It was a curious approach to life for self-styled leftist revolutionaries, but cocaine and politics had long since cut a merger in Colombia. In the autumn of 1985 guerrillas from the M-19 commando squad had stormed the nation's highest court, slaughtering more than eighty people—including eleven Supreme Court justices—before they were rooted out and killed themselves. Another year elapsed before investigative journalists discovered that the raid had been conceived and financed by a ranking member of the native drug cartel in order to intimidate the court and trash incriminating documents from secret files.

The men whom Bolan sought this morning were contemporaries of those M-19 commandos. Most of them had joined the movement at an early age, defecting when their trusted leadership was decimated at the Palace of Justice in

1985. A dozen spin-off "armies" had been organized within six months, the bulk of them suppressed by DAS security police before they had a chance to put down roots. The People's Army of Colombia had proven themselves more durable, survivors in a nation under siege, where mere continuation of existence was a victory of sorts.

Two nights earlier a group of American journalists reporting on the drug wars was machine-gunned in a local bar, with several persons killed and others gravely wounded. "Credit" for the raid was shortly claimed by spokesmen for the People's Army, edging out the rabid competition in a bid for notoriety.

The story might have ended there, for all intents and purposes, except that Bolan knew enough to look behind the scenes. His sources told him that the PAC was bought and paid for, leaders thriving on the payroll of the drug cartel while members of the rank and file obeyed their orders down the line, believing their acts of savagery would somehow benefit a nonexistent "people's revolution."

Any way you sliced it, they were mercenary guns for hire, and it was time for them to pay.

In addition to Bolan's stock two hundred pounds, he carried side arms—the Beretta 93-R and the mighty Desert Eagle, in their separate rigs—as well as an Uzi submachine gun, several fragmentation and stun grenades, plus extra magazines for both his pistols and the compact stuttergun.

Twelve feet across and seven stories down.

No time to waste.

The Executioner made a running start and cleared the alley with an easy yard to spare. Before the muscle tremors in his legs and back had faded, he keyed the compact walkie-talkie and announced, "I'm over. Moving in."

Below him, on the gritty streets, the men of Phoenix Force would read that message loud and clear. He pictured Katzenelenbogen and the others checking out their watches, counting down the ninety seconds they'd chosen as an arbitrary lull before making contact with the enemy.

From that point on the ground troops would be kicking ass.

The choice of targets was ideal from Bolan's point of view—no innocent civilians in the way when it was time to engage battle. Sex and age aside, the building's covert occupants were hard-core revolutionaries, one and all. They stood together in a crunch, when there was wet work to perform, and they could die that way, as well.

Their deaths would send a little message to Luis Costanza and his bosom friends in the cartel, reminding them of Bolan's law: for every action on the street, they could expect equal commensurate reactions.

Blood for blood.

A cleansing flame to scourge the enemy.

The door was locked, but Bolan's handy set of picks released the latch in something under thirty seconds flat. Below him, stairs and musty darkness offered nothing to suggest that the middle floor was occupied by self-styled warriors in a rebel cause.

But he could feel their presence all the same.

He flicked the Uzi's safety off and started down.

WITH THIRTY SECONDS down and counting, Jack Grimaldi cleared the basement steps and tried the door, immediately reaching for his pry bar when he found it locked. There might be sentries in the basement, even an alarm, but he was betting the soldiers of the People's Army trusted in their cover and the lookout they'd posted on the street.

Removing that particular obstruction would be Katzenelenbogen's problem. As for Grimaldi, his mission was to penetrate the basement, make his way upstairs and lend a hand if things got messy.

Which they could, and no mistake.

Their risks were doubled on a daylight raid in Medellín, regardless of the neighborhood. Police wouldn't respond as quickly to reports of trouble here as in a neighborhood where wealth dictated the priorities, but they'd still turn out.

With the epic violence of the past few days in mind, they'd be turning out well armed, prepared to kill.

The basement smelled of rot and rodents, and there were scratchy-scuffling noises in the darkness that told the Stony Man pilot he wasn't alone. He thought about the different horror movies he'd seen in younger days, with swarms of rats devouring their human prey alive, and felt the short hairs rising on his neck until he palmed the flashlight, found the switch and flicked it on.

More scuffling came from the shadows, safe beyond the cone of light he generated, and Grimaldi saw the ruby glint of eyes between the stacks of moldy packing crates and shrouded stacks of furniture. Beneath his jacket, in a leather swivel sling, the Ingram submachine gun was a reassuring presence, giving him an edge in case the rats decided he was brunch.

Intent on watching where he put his feet, Grimaldi missed the hanging cobwebs until they were in his face, a veil of gossamer that left his fingers sticky to the touch.

Terrific. Rats *and* spiders.

Muttering a curse, Grimaldi found the stairs and mounted them. Another locked door stood at the top, but this one had a dead bolt that was easily opened from the inside. He turned it, one hand on the knob and one hand on the Ingram as he waited, counting down the doomsday numbers in his head.

One man was out front, for sure. If he had backup they were unaware of, Grimaldi would figure on the lobby or the stairs leading to the second floor. In either case, a man or two with automatic weapons could delay invaders long enough for their companions to escape across the network of adjacent rooftops.

Once he emerged from the apartment building's basement, it was thin ice all the way.

So what else was new?

It had been thin ice, one way or another, since Grimaldi had joined the Executioner's crusade against the Mafia. It had been another life, a different time and place, but he'd never once regretted the irrevocable choice. There had been pain and loss along the way, damn right, but any way you edged around the subject, that was part of life. How many people had the opportunity to leave a mark and count for something in the time it took their orbits to decay?

A few.

In retrospect Grimaldi knew he wouldn't have had it any other way.

No watchdogs waited in the lobby as he stepped across the threshold with the Ingram braced against his hip. The walls were moldy and graffiti stained, the lobby carpet threadbare, torn in places to reveal concrete beneath. Grimaldi circled toward the stairs, with one eye on the sunlit street.

If Katz was running late, there could be problems with the outside man. A firefight on the sidewalk meant potential chaos, with their targets on the move before they had a chance to spring the trap.

He checked the empty stairwell and the one landing he could see, then doubled back across the lobby toward the doors. The glass was papered over with official condemnation notices and warnings not to trespass on the premises, but there was still ample space for a pedestrian to glance inside and spot the gringo with a submachine gun in his hand.

And what would happen then?

In Medellín, where each new day meant ten more murders in the streets, a witness might decide to yell for the police or to keep his mouth shut, based on personal priorities. Involvement with the law meant media exposure, and you never knew exactly who was checking out the headlines with an eye toward possible revenge.

Grimaldi pressed his face against the glass and looked in both directions, turning quickly so that the stairs were left unguarded for only a moment. If the sentry was in place, he must have shifted down the block, beyond Grimaldi's line of vision. Or maybe Katz had made the tag already, waiting for the next step on Grimaldi's end.

He turned the bolt and grimaced at the sharp sound of the lock. A second mechanism near the floor resisted until he let the Ingram dangle on its sling and used both hands.

All clear.

The Stony Man pilot's mission didn't call for him to stand and wait. Somewhere above him Bolan was descending on the enemy alone, one man against a dozen, maybe twice that number if the rebels had a thing for hiding out in groups. The Phoenix team could make their own time coming in, but Grimaldi was on his way.

One glance told him the elevator was a write-off, not that he'd trust it in the present circumstances, anyway. The stairs were hazardous enough, without Grimaldi popping out of nowhere on a floor the enemy had occupied and turned into a home away from home.

Grimaldi kept the Ingram up and ready as he climbed, each landing a potential ambush if the rebels had another sentry posted. One false move, one creaking step, and he was history. He wouldn't have a chance to turn and run before a shotgun blast or stream of automatic gunfire came blazing down the staircase in response to any noise.

The good news was a distant, muffled engine sputtering above him, probably a compact generator to provide the rebel troops with light and juice to run their hot plates while they hid out in the rotting tenement. It would be a bit of cover for his footsteps as he climbed.

His heart was pounding, and his shirt was plastered to his ribs with perspiration, when he leveled off on three. Two flights, an easy ten or fifteen seconds if he hurried, and the People's Army would be open to attack. He knew Bolan should be ready for his push by now, prepared to close the back door and prevent their quarry from slipping out.

But where the hell was Phoenix Force?

A sound of footsteps echoed on the stairs behind him, down on two. There was no time for second-guessing as the clock ran down, Grimaldi realizing he was either trapped or reinforced. Whichever, his response would be the same.

Straight forward, down the dragon's throat.

There *was* a sentry, but Grimaldi caught him in the middle of a daydream, scratching at his crotch through faded denims that had gone too long without a wash. The young man heard him coming, but it was too late.

Grimaldi saw the guy's shotgun propped against the wall, the automatic pistol tucked inside the lookout's belt. Neither one could help him now as the Ingram ripped parabellum manglers in a ragged line across his chest from left to right. The jarring impact hurled him backward, boot heels drumming on the moldy carpet as he fell.

Voices came from behind Grimaldi and below, and he thought he recognized Encizo and maybe Calvin James. After a few more strides, there was only time to think about surviving as he held the Ingram's trigger down and swept the corridor in a tight figure eight.

ONE THING about a neighborhood where half the buildings were condemned, thought Yakov Katzenelenbogen, was that it cut down on witnesses. Of course, he knew that several of the "vacant" tenements and shops were occupied by squatters, hiding from the landlords and police, but their illegal status only helped. They'd be less inclined to call for the authorities, especially since most of the abandoned flats had no electric power, much less working telephones.

Downrange, a sentry lit a cigarette and scanned the soccer scores in *El Tiempo,* lounging on the stoop and acting casual. He had a short run to the double doors, if anything went wrong—three concrete steps, and two more healthy strides beyond—but there would be a panic button somewhere, safely out of sight. A radio perhaps, or—

Bolan's voice distracted Katz before he could complete the thought.

"I'm over. Moving in."

That gave them ninety seconds to eliminate the sentry, make their way inside and join the Executioner on four. No time to waste, but the Israeli kept his seat behind the rented compact's steering wheel. Beside him, Calvin James might easily have been a figure etched from stone.

Five seconds later Rafael Encizo captured their attention, weaving down the sidewalk in a drunken stagger, mumbling to himself and searching through the pockets of his tattered army surplus jacket like a man who had misplaced his keys or cigarettes. The sentry saw him coming, glancing up from *El Tiempo* long enough to satisfy himself there was nothing to be feared. Another drunk or junkie looking for a place to hide and sleep the day away, emerging after dusk to feed the monkey on his back.

A few yards short of where the lookout sat, Encizo stumbled, dropping to all fours. He cursed and struck the sun-bleached pavement with his fist, the right hand ducking back inside his jacket and emerging with a pistol weighted by the bulky outline of a silencer.

One shot was all it took at fifteen feet, but Encizo used two, a hedge against mistakes. Before the sentry's blood could pool and dribble off the step beneath his shattered skull, the gruff Israeli and his comrade were in motion, racing for the stoop to help Encizo hoist the corpse and drag it out of sight.

A half block down, the children were distracted by their games, oblivious to sudden death around them. Katz tried the double doors with all their warning signs and found them open, pushing through and waiting while the corpse was pulled inside. He locked the doors behind them, checked his watch and nodded toward the stairs. "Come on."

With Bolan and Grimaldi, they were five against unknown odds. Two other members of the Phoenix team—McCarter and Manning—were stationed on adjoining roofs across the street, prepared to cover a retreat if things went sour on the raid.

Assuming there was anyone alive to need their help.

"That's sixty seconds," Calvin James announced, his voice a breathless whisper as they reached the stairs.

Katz led, an Uzi submachine gun in his hand, the others following in single file and hanging back a bit to frustrate any snipers they encountered on the way. If one went down, at least the other two would have a fleeting opportunity to save themselves.

One landing, and the tough Israeli braced his weapon's muzzle with the stainless-steel prosthesis that replaced his right hand. No action or resistance confronted them as they quickly scanned the second floor, all brooding shadows with the power off, and darkness filling up the space where lights once burned around the clock.

So far, so good.

They were climbing, finally picking up some time, when Katz heard the scuffling feet above them, followed by a muffled curse and sudden automatic fire. It was an Ingram by the sound of it, so rapid that the rounds went off like canvas ripping in a gale-force wind.

Grimaldi? Or perhaps Grimaldi going down?

"On me!" he snapped and took the final staircase in a rush, the way his troops had once stormed Syrian positions in the Golan Heights.

It was a case of all or nothing, do or die, the only way Katz knew how to play the game.

THE SUDDEN BURST of gunfire made up Bolan's mind. He had no way of knowing whether it was Jack Grimaldi or Phoenix Force engaging their opponents, but it scarcely mattered, either way.

Nine seconds early, and he had to move.

A pair of rebel gunmen occupied the fourth-floor landing just below him, lounging in the semidarkness, totally oblivious to Bolan's presence on the stairs. He'd descended quietly and was close enough to smell them. Infrequent bathing was apparently the price of doing business in condemned establishments.

Instead of trying to convert the fourth-floor wiring, Bolan's enemies had strung their own along the corridor and through connected rooms, dim bulbs providing faint illumination reminiscent of the safety lighting in a sewer. There was something of a sewer fragrance, too, and Bolan guessed the rebels were answering assorted calls of nature on the lower floors, where toilets starved for water would no longer flush.

The unexpected gunfire brought the two young men to their feet, one reaching for a pistol on his hip. Bolan hit both with a burst while their eyes and minds were focused on the far end of the corridor. They fell together, stunned expressions on their faces, murky crimson soaking through the carpet underneath.

He hit the landing in a combat crouch and risked a glance around the corner, ducking back before a well-placed round sprayed plaster dust into the air. It had been enough to show him muzzle-flashes at the end of the corridor, with rebels spilling out of rooms on both sides. No head count, but a single glance had shown him that the self-styled revolutionaries had his troop outnumbered three or four to one.

Bolan palmed a stun grenade and yanked the safety pin, already counting as he pitched it blindly around the corner with a sidearm toss.

Five seconds.

Huddled with his back against the wall, he closed his eyes and clutched the Uzi tighter, waiting for the semidarkness to explode in blinding light.

3

In retrospect Grimaldi thought it must have been dumb luck that let him spot the stun grenade. He had a running target in his sights when Bolan ripped his adversaries at the far end of the corridor, and he was ready when the warrior made his pitch. Grimaldi saw the olive drab cylinder complete one full rotation in its flight before he jostled Katz and his companions back toward the stairs.

"Grenade!" he snapped. "Get down!"

The "flash-bang" tag applied to stun grenades by troopers in the British SAS was perfectly appropriate. A blinding pulse of light disoriented the intended targets, while concussion left them deafened and semiconscious, sometimes with their eardrums torn.

This time it nearly worked.

Grimaldi came up firing in the aftermath of the explosion, ears still ringing as he cut down two rebels from fifteen feet away. It only took a glance for him to realize that some of their antagonists were down and out, while distance from the blast had cushioned others, leaving them in different stages of preparedness to fight. A third wave, still emerging from the open rooms, seemed largely unaffected by the stun grenade.

Grimaldi emptied his Ingram with a rising burst that swept another member of the People's Army off his feet, then scrambled back to cover while he ditched the empty magazine and snapped a fresh one in its place. Around him Katz, James and Encizo poured automatic fire into the rebel lines, selecting random targets as they fought to clear the hall.

By now the rebels were returning fire in both directions, concentrating on Grimaldi's end, where they were faced with four guns as opposed to Bolan's one. They'd assume the attackers were police and would fight with everything they had to keep from winding up in prison, or in front of a firing squad.

But still no scurry to escape.

Grimaldi tugged at Katz's sleeve. "Did anybody check the floor below?"

"What for?"

And then it dawned on Katz, the same way it had struck Grimaldi, out of nowhere, like a hammer stroke between the eyes.

Was it imagination, or were fewer rebels firing back along the left side of the corridor? How many had been killed or wounded to account for dropouts from the fight? Was there an escape hatch cut between the floors to help the rebels slip away?

"I'll check it out," James said.

Encizo fell back to follow as the black man started downstairs, their clomping footsteps covered by the sound of gunfire.

Grimaldi cursed himself for not considering the possibility before. It stood to reason that the People's Army would prepare an alternate escape route to allow for raids against their makeshift field command post. Cut off from the stairs and fire escape, the only way for them to go was down.

Too late?

The pilot kept his fingers crossed and prayed the Phoenix warriors weren't charging toward a hornet's nest. If members of the rebel force could exit one floor down, they might attack Katz and Grimaldi from behind instead of breaking for the street.

But there was no time for dwelling on the gloomy options as a pair of rebel gunners broke from cover on the right, advancing on the staircase, laying down a screen of cover fire. Grimaldi swung his Ingram into target acquisition, snarling as he held the trigger down and emptied the clip.

IT GALLED Calvin James that he hadn't thought about a safety hatch—that no one had—but they were all so caught up in the hasty preparations for a clean assault that it had fallen through the cracks. His Navy SEAL instructors would have taken him to task, but criticism only counted if the object was alive.

And it was still too close to call.

His weapon was the stubby MP-5K submachine gun, manufactured by Heckler & Koch as the "baby" of their MP series. Measuring less than thirteen inches overall, it offered the same cyclic fire rate as the full-size model, spewing 9 mm parabellums at an average speed of eight hundred rounds per minute. The little subgun burned up 30-round box magazines as if they were going out of style, but James was carrying a dozen extra.

He heard Rafael Encizo on his heels. It made good sense to use a backup gunner on a run like this when facing unknown odds, but James was still concerned about the men upstairs. Sheer numbers gave the rebel troops a decent chance of breaking out, and there was nothing he could do about it now. Except to slam the back door—if there *was* a back door—on retreating enemies.

A rebel met them on the third-floor landing, brandishing a riot shotgun, but his aim was off. The buckshot whispered over Calvin's head and blasted moldy plaster from the wall. Momentum kept him moving as he squeezed the trigger on his stubby H&K, delivering a chest-high burst without a break in stride.

The gunner vaulted backward, dying on his feet before he had a chance to work the shotgun's slide. James flattened against the wall, Encizo on his left, and they could hear excited voices in the corridor.

Four gunners by the sound of it, and more if some of them were keeping their opinions to themselves.

"On three."

Encizo nodded, standing with his feet on different steps, the Uzi braced against his hip.

Their only hope was speed and sheer audacity. Surprise had vanished with the point man's death, and James was painfully aware that he was volunteering for the role of moving target in a narrow shooting gallery. If there was any viable alternative, he'd have snapped it up, but there was no spare time to ponder while their enemies retreated toward the other stairwell.

"One."

The H&K felt heavy in his hands, a function of the stress that set his nerves on edge.

"Two."

He tensed, ready for action.

"Three!"

James lunged forward in a power slide, the MP-5K spitting death at shadows in the murky corridor. Encizo ripped off half a magazine before the snipers drove him back, while James slithered across the carpet on his belly, rolling into cover on the other side. He seemed surprised to find that he was still alive.

"God *damn!*"

He palmed a frag grenade and held it up for Rafael to see. The Cuban grinned and nodded, digging for munitions of his own. They yanked the pins together, Calvin giving the signal with a nod. Encizo had to make his pitch left-handed, but he never missed a beat.

The double blast whipped up a dust cloud in the corridor, releasing streams of plaster from the walls and ceiling. Somewhere in the middle of it Calvin heard a young voice crying out in pain, a desperate, hurting sound that left him cold.

Screw sympathy. These bastards committed murder in the name of politics and bragged about it afterward.

He moved before the shrapnel finished plunking holes in rotten walls, a crouching shadow, with a stream of bullets from the MP-5K opening the way. Encizo overtook him in the first few strides, his Uzi keeping time.

They had one job: to slam the back door on their enemies and nail it shut.

James meant to see it done, or die.

MACK BOLAN FOLLOWED UP the stun grenade with a sustained burst, already moving as the first concussive echoes died away. In front of him he counted a half-dozen rebels stretched out on the floor or reeling drunkenly across his field of fire, stone deaf and blinded by the flash, unable to defend themselves.

He cut them down.

Reloading on the run, he made the nearest doorway, pushing through and flattening himself against the wall inside. A flitting shadow brought the Uzi back to life, a short burst knocking divots in the wall to Bolan's left. Or what remained of it.

A gaping hole, six feet across and roughly seven feet in height, connected one room with the next where hammers had been used to smash a makeshift door. It was a half-assed job, discarded chunks of plasterboard and mortar heaped up on the floor on either side, but it was functional—a runway between adjoining rooms.

If the rebels cared enough to link these two, it stood to reason that the other rooms had also been connected, probably on both sides of the corridor.

As Bolan braced himself to check the aperture, an automatic rifle poked around the corner, hosing down the room with random fire. He hit the floor and rolled, acquiring his target just in time to see the piece withdrawn.

The assailant would have to check his handiwork or fire again. There was no way any terrorist with half a brain could sit back and let it go at that.

More shadows moved on the far side of the open wall, the light bulbs their undoing. The warrior had the Uzi braced and ready when a young face edged around the ragged wall.

A 3-round burst ripped through the spotter's forehead from a range of fifteen feet, his cranium erupting in a crimson halo as he dropped back out of sight. Before the other rebels could decide on a response, the frag grenade was palmed and primed, an easy sidearm pitch dropping it just beyond the makeshift door.

A smoky thunderclap extinguished lights in the adjoining room, and ringing silence took the place of frightened voices. Bolan scrambled to his feet and followed in a rush, the Uzi tracking as he counted lifeless bodies on the floor.

In the wall directly opposite was another hole, as if a giant ram had pierced the room on one side and continued out the other, leaving only rubble in its wake. A stray round whispered through the opening and struck somewhere behind the Executioner, far enough off target that it didn't count.

The warrior sidestepped and risked a quick glance through the rough-hewn portal. For an instant he imagined he was looking down the building's throat, a tunnel cut from east to west, traversing the entire fourth floor. He was reminded of the baffles in a firearms silencer, or locks in a canal.

Downrange, two rooms ahead of him, a solitary figure surfaced, sighting down the barrel of an M-16. The Executioner squeezed off a nasty burst and leapt aside before the 5.56 mm tumblers started chewing up his private space.

Another frag grenade?

It seemed too far for him to make the pitch with any kind of accuracy, and he couldn't follow through regardless while the intervening room lay unsecured. For all he knew there could be a half-dozen rebels waiting for him just beyond the open wall.

So, first things first.

Bolan took a breath and held it, counting down the numbers as he braced himself to sweep the room next door. Then he made his move, a long dive through the portal, rolling over once before he came up firing at the two men in the room. They should have been expecting him, but they were sluggish off the mark, their trigger fingers frozen in surprise. The warrior stitched them with a blazing figure eight and spun to face a hulking shadow in the doorway, hesitating long enough to verify the presence of an enemy.

The rebel had a cut above one eye, and half his face was streaked with blood, but it didn't appear to slow him down. He entered firing an AK-47, bullets ripping through the wall a foot above the warrior's head.

The Uzi stuttered in reply, the magazine exhausted after a half-dozen rounds. But it was all he needed. Bolan watched the rebel stagger, going down with crimson blotches soaking through his khaki shirt.

Ahead of him the firing had intensified. Another frag grenade went off and rattled plaster from the walls. He knew the hellish racket must be audible outside. How long before the squatters in adjacent tenements got angry or scared enough to try to find a telephone?

No time to waste.

Reloading on the move, he estimated six or seven rooms remaining on the left-hand side before that portion of the floor was cleared. He should meet Jack Grimaldi and the men of Phoenix Force somewhere along the way—if any of them got that far.

Dismissing thoughts of death and failure, Bolan concentrated on his goal. *Someone* was fighting at the far end of the corridor and could use his help. The Executioner continued his blitzkrieg.

AS RAFAEL ENCIZO followed Calvin James into the cloud of battle smoke, the last thing on his mind was taking prisoners. Their mission had been simple and direct: eradicate this outpost of the People's Army and prevent the terrorists on hand from claiming any future lives.

The order meant exactly what it said.

Destruction.

Scorched earth all the way.

The frag grenades had flattened several men, but three or four were sprinting for the other staircase, racing for their lives. James ripped a couple of them with his H&K, the others scattering to rooms on both sides of the hallway, returning fire as they went to ground.

Encizo found an open doorway on his right and ducked inside, stray bullets splintering the frame behind him and furrowing the walls. Across the hall and one door farther down James was reloading.

A stalemate spelled disaster, pinning down both sides until police or troops arrived to block the streets. It would be better if the handful of surviving rebels slipped away, a treat for Manning and McCarter with their sniper scopes.

But giving up had never been Encizo's strong point, whether he was training for a raid or marking time in Castro's prison system, living hand to mouth and day by day. Survival of the fittest meant no quitters need apply, and the wily Cuban was accustomed to confronting killer odds.

The numbers weren't so bad—in fact, he thought they must be nearly even—but a rush along the open corridor was tantamount to suicide. If there had only been some other way...

The thin grate covering a heater vent was mounted in the farthest corner from the door. Encizo measured with his hands and decided it was wide enough to let him pass if he could only reach that high.

The solitary piece of furniture remaining in the room was a decrepit armchair, ripped in places, with the moldy stuffing on display. He dragged it over, wedged it in the corner and made certain it would hold his weight before he made the climb.

A moment working with his clasp knife, and the grating lay discarded on the floor. Encizo stretched to place his submachine gun in the air shaft, pushing it away from him to clear a path. Soft cobwebs brushed against his hand and set his teeth on edge.

No turning back.

The first lunge was a killer, but he managed, digging with his elbows, cursing as the sharp edge of the open vent left scratches on his chest and ribs. There was a momentary hesitation while he cleared his belt, then his outstretched fingers found the Uzi, clutching it for the elusive feeling of security it gave.

Encizo wormed his way along the air shaft on his belly, brushing dusty webs aside and passing three more vents before he reached the small apartment he was looking for. Sharp cordite from below assailed his nostrils, and the echo of sporadic gunfire hammered his ears. By twisting on his side, he glimpsed two rebels at the doorway, taking turns as each one fired a burst along the hall, then ducked back to let the other take his place.

He tried the grate and felt it shift, but not enough. The screws weren't designed to be released from this side of the trap, and he'd have to find another way without surrendering too much of his surprise advantage to the enemy.

His mind made up, Encizo palmed a stun grenade and pulled the pin, his right hand groping for the Browning automatic pistol in its shoulder rigging. Two shots ought to do the job, if he was accurate enough.

Encizo grimaced as he thought about the noise, but there was nothing he could use for earplugs, no more precious time to waste. He estimated the location of the screws that held the grate in place, squeezed off a single round at each of them and dropped his flash-bang as the metal plate fell free.

The blast was merciless in spite of Rafael's abrupt retreat and the arms wrapped tight around his head. His ears were throbbing as he scuttled forward, plunging headfirst through the grate, already firing as he dropped into the room.

His targets barely felt the bullets ripping into them and snuffing out their lives. Across the hall another pair of rebels lost it in the sudden rage and panic of the moment, bursting out of cover with their submachine guns spitting aimless fire in all directions. Encizo dropped one in his tracks, and James tagged the other with a rising burst that lifted him completely off his feet before it set him down again.

And they were done.

Almost.

Retreating toward the stairs and their companions on the floor above, Encizo caught a hint of movement through an open doorway on his left. He followed through in time to see a pair of denim legs descending through a hole cut in the ceiling, wrapped around a length of knotted rope. Another moment and the rebel's torso followed, then his head. A shock of dusty hair fell around his shoulders, and a rifle was strapped across his back.

Encizo could have killed him then, but something made him hesitate. He took another step into the room and met the rebel as he landed, turned and reached back to free his weapon from its sling.

The muzzle of the Cuban's submachine gun cracked against the guy's skull and took him down. Encizo took a moment to relieve him of his weapon, then dragged him through the door and out into the hall.

"What's this?" James asked.

"A prisoner."

"Who needs it?"

"We might, if we want to prove who's picking up the tab."

"You're still in doubt?"

"The press might be. A word from this guy, with reporters dead, it just might be enough to turn the heat up on Costanza from another side."

"Your call," James said. "I'll help you drag him to the stairs, but if he tries to fuck us up, I'm gonna waste his ass."

HIS ENEMIES HAD DRAWN together in the last three rooms, and they were laying down a heavy cover fire as Bolan psyched himself up for one more push. There were at least eight guns, and probably a dozen, but their concentration was divided now, with Phoenix and Grimaldi pinning down the other flank. If it came down to breaking out, they'd be coming Bolan's way. A dozen guns against his one, and there was no way he could take them all.

The obvious solution, then, was to annihilate the enemy before they dredged up nerve enough to make that charge.

The Executioner's last frag grenade was in his hand and the pin discarded as he circled wide around the room, approaching the contested portal on his belly. Automatic fire had sieved the walls around him, showering the floor with chips of masonry that rasped and grated under Bolan as he crawled along.

When he was close enough, he shifted the grenade and let the spoon pop free, already counting down the seconds as he wound up for the pitch. Five seconds shaved to three, with no chance of a comeback as he lobbed the deadly egg and ducked back under cover to wait for the blast.

A bloody scarecrow staggered into view, his left arm hanging by a shred of flesh, his right hand wrapped around an automatic pistol. Bolan dropped him with a short precision burst and stepped around the falling body, firing left and right across the threshold and into the adjacent room. The frag grenade had done its job, but two or three of his opponents still showed signs of life. The Uzi stifled their cries.

Next door the firing sputtered to a halt, and Bolan poised himself, prepared to answer any challenge from the enemy. Instead, he recognized the face of Yakov Katzenelenbogen peering at him through the smoke and dust.

"All finished there?" the gruff Israeli asked.

"Looks like."

"In that case I believe we should be on our way."

Emerging from the charnel house with Katz, Bolan found Grimaldi covering the silent corridor. "The rest?"

"Right here," another voice informed him, reaching Bolan from the stairs.

Three faces confronted him—Calvin James and Rafael Encizo, with a bloodied stranger in between.

"Explain."

"Consider him a present," the Cuban said. "Wind him up, he sings a song you may enjoy."

The Executioner allowed himself a cautious smile. "I might at that."

4

They played a hunch and tried the penthouse, overlooking Bay Front Park on Biscayne Boulevard. The doorman started to protest, but Turrin's federal badge helped turn his attitude around. On second thought he did recall a visitor to Mr. Constantine's apartment. Miss Loughlin. Yes, she was a regular. And, no, she hadn't left as yet.

It took a special elevator key to reach the penthouse, and the doorman gave his up without complaint, accepting Turrin's sage advice that it would be unwise to phone ahead and warn the lady company was on the way.

"I love it," Blancanales muttered as they waited for the elevator. "First she blows the whistle on him, then she drops around to clean him out."

"Guy must have pissed her off," Schwarz replied.

"He won't do that again."

"If she's running with a lawyer," Turrin said, "my guess would be that she knows her rights."

Politician pinned him with a stony glance. "What rights are those?"

The man from Justice knew how Blancanales felt. Their link with Lyons dated from the early days of Bolan's war against the Mafia, around L.A., when Lyons was a young detective working on the LAPD "hardcase" unit, squaring off against the mob. It was impossible for any of them to predict the paths their separate lives would take...or how they'd be forged into a single fighting unit over time.

Strange days, but they were pledged to one another now, more intimate than lovers in their way. Blood spilled and danger shared formed a bond that only death could break.

He thought of Lyons stretched out in a box and tasted bitter rage.

What rights are those?

No rights at all.

The elevator brought them to a stylish vestibule, complete with potted palms and abstract artwork on the walls. The single door in front of them was solid oak, hand-carved—and standing open. Poised upon the threshold was the kind of woman who could grace the cover of a fashion magazine or pose for raunchy centerfolds, with no apparent contradiction in between. She had a hand-tooled leather suitcase in her hand, a glossy mink across her shoulder and a stunned expression on her face.

"Miss Sheila Loughlin?" Blancanales asked.

"Yes?"

"We need to have a talk."

"I'm sorry," she began, "I really can't—"

"I'll bet you can," Blancanales interrupted. He took the suitcase from her hand and edged her back inside the penthouse, Schwarz and Leo bringing up the rear.

The living room was half again as large as the apartment Turrin and his wife had occupied during their final year of college. Spacious bedrooms opened off one side, a dining room and kitchen on the other. From the door he had a glimpse of massive sliding windows fronting on a balcony, the sea beyond.

"I've got a flight to catch," the lady told them, trying hard to let her indignation triumph over fear.

"You missed it," Schwarz replied.

"Who *are* you?"

"That depends. Play straight and tell us what we need to know, and we just might be the only friends you've got."

"If you're from the police—"

"Did anybody mention the police?"

Her face went pale. "What, then?"

"We just dropped by your boyfriend's boat," Turrin said.

"Alex? You can save your breath. He's not my boyfriend anymore. In case you hadn't guessed, I'm moving out."

"Too late, I'd say. He had a little accident."

She didn't want to ask, but it was unavoidable. "What kind of accident?"

"Some trouble shaving." Blancanales drew an index finger left to right across his throat. "It's hard to figure how he did it, tied up in that chair the way he was."

"Oh, God."

"You didn't know?"

"How could I?"

Turrin shrugged. "A little birdie tells me you've been making calls."

She froze, trembling like a rabbit in the middle of the highway, trapped, with headlights bearing down. "I asked you once—"

"We're not Colombians, okay? If we were interested in killing anybody, you'd be dead by now."

"I made one call," she said, a tremor in her voice. "Just one."

"To the DEA?"

Turrin saw the lady weighing her responses, balancing the truth against a hasty lie. If they turned out to be Costanza's men, admission of a link with the authorities would seal her fate, but she had leaked too much already. There would be no turning back.

"That's right," she told them.

"We didn't get to him in time."

"I see." The lady let her shoulders slump, retreating to a chair. The tailored skirt rode up her thighs as she sat down, and Turrin dragged his eyes back to her face.

It wouldn't hurt to let her think they represented the DEA. If there were any comebacks down the line, somebody else could sort it out. "You strike me as the kind who plans ahead," he told her.

Staring back at Turrin with a dead look in her eyes, she asked, "Is that supposed to be a compliment?"

"An observation. Something tells me you were pissed off at Constantine, the way he shined you on." Pure guesswork now, but judging by the grim expression on her face, he had the right idea.

"So what?" she asked.

"So maybe you took out a little health insurance. Just in case his playmates started thinking of you as a liability."

"I don't know what you mean."

"Too bad. We had in mind to let you walk, if you could put us on the right track. I guess we'll have to sort it out downtown." He glanced at Schwarz and Blancanales. "What's the deal, accessory to murder one?"

"Sounds good to me," Blancanales said.

"Hold on a second! Why would I call up the DEA if I was in on having Alex killed?"

Turrin looked her in the eye. "First glance, it makes a decent alibi."

"You're wrong."

"I guess we'll let the jury make that call."

"What do you want?"

"The counselor was working for Luis Costanza. Ring a bell?"

"It might."

"His contact in Miami was a woman. She's the one we're looking for."

"That's it?"

"Could be."

She reached inside her purse and came out with an address book—initials A.C. on the cover, gold on black. "He liked to write things down. I guess it didn't help him much."

"It might help someone else," Turrin replied, thumbing back to *T* and skimming down the page. "You never know."

"I CAN'T BELIEVE she gave him the directions," Blancanales said.

"We won't know till we check it out," Schwarz said. "Anyway, she didn't have to *give* it to him. Guys like that, they pin things down. They're always looking for an edge."

"He found a sharp one this time."

"Yeah, and it breaks my heart."

"It might be nothing," Turrin cautioned from the back seat. "Unlisted phone, the 'M.T.' could be anybody."

"It's a place to start," Schwarz said. "If you've got something better . . ."

"No," Turrin allowed.

"So we can check it out at least. It's not like we were booked up for the day."

"I just hate wasting time, you know?"

"It's only wasted if we're sitting on our butts and doing nothing when we could be on the street."

"Okay."

They traveled north on Ludlam to the Tamiami Trail, then west again until they left the city behind. Beyond Sweetwater it was plain old Highway 41, and they were cruising at a steady sixty-five across the Everglades. Dark water, reeds and floating islands stretched off on either side as far as you could see.

"How far until we hit Monroe?" Schwarz asked.

"Another twenty, give or take," Turrin replied.

Schwarz scanned the open highway and surrounding marshland with a brooding frown. "We stand out like a goddamn horsefly in a bowl of cream."

"The boat was too damn risky," Blancanales countered. "They could hear us coming from a mile away."

"If anybody's there."

"And if they're not, it doesn't matter that they're obvious."

"So what's the deal again?" Schwarz asked.

"Beyond Monroe, the next road on our left," Turrin said. "Three-quarters of a mile from there."

"We have to figure guards beyond the highway."

"Maybe make a drive-by. If we have to, leave the car back in Monroe and find another way from there."

"Sounds fair."

"You think they'd have a spotter in the town?"

"Depends on how secure the lady feels."

"Some lady."

"Right."

Monroe was nothing but a wide place in the road, a pit stop rescued from the swamp that featured gas pumps and a burger grill, a bait shop, and skiffs and airboats rented by the hour or the day.

"Hang on. What's this?" Schwarz asked.

They almost missed the access road, despite three pairs of vigilant eyes. It was secured with a chain, unmarked, and someone had attempted to disguise the entrance with a screen of shrubbery.

"So much for driving in," Turrin said.

Schwarz motored on another mile before he turned around and started back in the direction of Monroe.

"The boats?" Blancanales asked.

"Unless you feel like wading in," Schwarz said.

"No thanks. I had a pair of alligator shoes one time. They're supposed to hold a grudge."

"No snakeskin belt?"

"That, too."

Schwarz forced a smile. "You're up shit creek, old buddy."

"You got that right."

They paid the day rate for a twelve-foot skiff with outboard motor and a pair of heavy oars. The local boy who took their money made no effort to conceal his skepticism as he looked them over, each in turn. "You're gonna ruin them city clothes."

"We brought a change," Schwarz replied, "if you've got somewhere we can go?"

"The crapper's round in back. That's all the changing room I got."

Ten minutes later, dressed in camouflage fatigues, they reassembled on the dock. Their military hardware and accessories weighed heavy in a pair of duffel bags that Schwarz and Turrin slung on shoulder straps.

"Y'all ain't hunters, I suppose?"

"Photographers," Schwarz answered, resting one hand on the duffel bag for emphasis. "We specialize in wildlife."

"Well, you come to the right place if you're looking for mosquitoes, anyway."

They used the outboard motor until the settlement was out of sight, then shut it down and fell back on the oars. Schwarz took the first round. Blancanales navigated in the bow, while Leo brought the automatic weapons out and got them loaded.

"Half a mile, you figure?" the Justice man asked.

"Give or take," Blancanales said.

"My aching back."

"You're getting old, is all."

"Damn right."

Another twenty minutes brought them to the trees, a vague facsimile of solid ground. There was no trace of sentries as they sloshed ashore and made the skiff secure.

"So far so good," Turrin said.

"So far," Schwarz corrected him, "we don't know if it's good or not."

They shouldered weapons, live rounds ready in the firing chambers to avoid unnecessary noise. Schwarz caught the heady fragrance of a flower he couldn't identify, but underneath it all there was the smell of rot. A scent of death. "Which way?" he asked.

Politician flashed a grim, ironic smile and pointed through the trees. "I make it dead ahead."

MARIA TERESINA LOVED the Everglades. In many ways the vast, uncharted wilderness reminded her of home, the tropic forests of Colombia. There were no mountains here, but she experienced a sense of kinship with the wildlife—birds and reptiles, larger predators.

She was a predator of sorts herself.

Maria knew that friends and enemies alike referred to her as La Araña, the Spider. Far from taking insult at the nickname, she regarded it as something of a compliment, a tribute to her way of doing business and disposing of competitors.

It was a reputation she could live with, even now, when she was under fire from every side.

Hostilities between Luis Costanza and his chief competitors—José Mercado and Raul Rodriguez—had begun the bloody cycle, with the Miami-Dade authorities mistaking the attacks on Maria as a natural reaction to her touted "antidrug crusade." It made her laugh, the ease with which such hardened champions of law and order were deceived . . . or paid to look the other way.

More recently the violence in Miami had appeared to emanate from other sources, which were unidentified. The problem grew more serious, the riddle more complex, when word came down from Medellín that her employer and his rivals had themselves been under siege, their private war indefinitely shelved while they closed ranks against a common enemy.

There was a common thread to all of this, and she'd been assigned to track it down. It was the kind of work she enjoyed, unmasking traitors, punishing their infidelity with fire and steel. She'd grown up with violence in Colombia and had earned a reputation on the streets of Medellín that made the bad boys step aside and let her pass. At first they treated her with abject fear, which soon matured into respect.

Respect and fear were a perfect combination in the netherworld of drugs and mayhem where Maria Teresina made her home.

She paced the long veranda, watching flocks of water-fowl in flight. Inside the house her men had taken off for lunch to let the captive catch his breath, but they'd soon be back at work.

Chad Lewis was the problem—one of them, at any rate—and on the fifth day of interrogation she was growing desperate to see him broken, spilling everything he knew to hold the pain at bay.

For openers she knew "Chad Lewis" was an alias, the first deception, which was swiftly followed by his lie about employment with the DEA. His bogus paperwork was all first-rate, the kind expected to be found on spooks or narcs with government connections, but Maria still had problems with the undercover-cop scenario.

Beginning with the local body count.

Whoever paid the freight, her newest enemies seemed more concerned with killing dealers than arresting them. It simply didn't jibe with anything Maria knew about the way a liberal government cracked down on crime. She was accustomed to committees and debates on television, raids and declarations of a brand-new "war on drugs" from every politician voted into office, trials that cost the government a fortune just to lock up some small-fry in Raiford for a year or two.

The government did *not* send shooters out to snuff the heavy movers in their homes and offices. It violated every rule and regulation in the books, and it would be too damn efficient for a pack of bureaucrats to buy the notion, anyway.

And yet . . .

The CIA had pulled some crazy stunts from time to time, assassinating heads of state and such. If she recalled her basic history, there had been rumors in the early seventies about domestic violence and the FBI, as well—some bombing incidents and left-wing radicals who turned up dead, presumably the victims of a power struggle in the ranks.

It wouldn't be the first time that a rogue department slipped its leash and launched a private war, but Lewis had been hanging tough so far. In spite of everything, they didn't even know his name.

The guy was hard, Maria had to give him that. His trim, athletic body bore the scars of past interrogations, wounds that would have killed a lesser man. He now had fresh scars to join the rest, and it had almost seemed a shame. Remembering the pleasure he'd given her in bed, Maria almost felt regret at the necessity of taking him apart.

Almost.

They'd been playing games so far—electric shocks, repeated workouts with the rubber hose and sandbag, pins and matches underneath his fingernails. She had to give him credit, though, especially for resistance to the drugs.

Most subjects would have folded when the chemicals kicked in, but Lewis had his act in gear. Maria didn't know if it was training or a simple strength of will peculiar to the man himself, but he'd talked in circles, going nowhere, to the point that her physician had refused to try another dose for fear that it would stop his heart.

Still, everybody had a breaking point. The proper strings had only to be jerked.

This afternoon they'd be shifting gears. There was a welding torch out back that might prove useful. She could find out how Chad Lewis took to being fried alive a square inch at a time. It promised to be educational.

Maria registered the birds before the blast.

One moment they were sitting in the trees and chattering to one another the way they always did; the next, a thunderclap of beating wings made her jump involuntarily. Her mind was reaching for an explanation when a car out front blew apart.

Shock waves rattled the windows in her house, oily smoke and leaping flames above the roofline catching on the lower limbs of overhanging trees.

The second car went up before her legs responded to a mental call for action, several windows shattering in the house this time. Her troops were spilling through the exits, front and back, as she ran to join them, calling for a weapon of her own.

Priorities.

If they couldn't interrogate their captive any longer, he must die. That done, it was Maria's duty to escape and save herself. Costanza was depending on her strength, her expertise, to keep the action rolling in Miami. There was nothing to be gained by standing fast and risking death or capture in a skirmish with their faceless enemies.

Somewhere beyond the house she picked up sounds of automatic gunfire and angry voices cursing, barking orders in the language of her homeland. On command one of her soldiers grudgingly surrendered his Beretta submachine gun, shifting anxiously from one foot to the other as Maria spelled out his orders. He'd go back inside the house and verify their captive's death before he slipped away.

Maria waited, watching him until he stepped inside the house, and then she bolted for the gravel drive. Two vehicles remained, both of them with keys in the ignition for a situation such as this. She chose a bronco for its four-wheel drive and slid behind the wheel, one hand on the ignition switch before she raised her eyes and saw the enemy.

He was an average man by all appearances, decked out in camouflage fatigues and sighting down the barrel of an M-16. His full attention was focused on Maria and the Bronco.

She recognized the 40 mm launcher mounted underneath the muzzle of the M-16 and saw her fate reflected in the stranger's eyes. She had perhaps a heartbeat in which to scoop up her submachine gun and fire a burst directly through the Bronco's windshield, praying for a lucky hit before he had a chance to fire.

Too late.

The world exploded in La Araña's face, a rush of hungry flames devouring her scream.

EMERGING FROM THE COVER of the tree line, Blancanales hosed the nearest gunners with a sustained burst. They might have known what hit them, but they never saw it coming, and the three of them went down together in a heap.

Around the front the echo of explosions told him Schwarz was on the job and kicking ass. Without their transport the Colombians would be forced to stand and fight or take their chances in the swamp. Meanwhile, the sound of automatic weapons on his other flank marked Turrin's entry to the battle, rounding off a classic pincer move.

Once they reached the house and grounds, it took about ten seconds to confirm the presence of their enemies. A pair of swarthy men were lounging on the porch in back, smoking weed, automatic rifles propped against the railing.

Some lookouts. They were the first to die when Blancanales opened fire.

A gunner emerged from the back door as the Able warrior reached the wooden stairs. They made each other at a glance, the short Colombian encumbered by a screen door swinging in his face. The first round from his .45 deflected into empty space. Politician hit him with a figure eight that drove him back across the threshold out of sight.

How many left inside? He couldn't risk a frag grenade to flush them out while there was any risk of Lyons being caught in the blast. Already flames were leaping at the front end of the house, and they were running out of time. The swamp would carry sounds of battle far and wide, alerting someone in Monroe. Response time for the nearest sheriff's unit would be slower, but they still couldn't afford the time to fool around.

He swung the screen aside and entered through a smallish kitchen, past the leaking body of his latest kill. More sounds of movement came from the far side of a swinging door, and Blancanales homed in on the noise, his submachine gun braced against one hip.

The two Colombians were stuffing ammo clips and plastic bags into a suitcase when Blancanales faced them down. The older of the pair clawed for a pistol tucked inside his belt, receiving a half-dozen parabellum shockers for his trouble. Thinking twice, the sidekick turned and ran, too slow to save himself as Blancanales emptied his magazine in one long burst.

Reloading on the move, he edged along an open hall with doors on both sides. The first stood open on an empty room, the second likewise, but the third was tightly closed. Beyond it he heard footsteps and a muffled cry of pain.

Blancanales didn't bother with the knob, relying on a swift kick with his weight behind it. Lyons sat naked in a chair, his wrists and ankles bound with duct tape, burns and bruises mottling his face and body from the hairline to the knees.

Beside him, frozen like a statue with a long knife in his hand, the slim Colombian was thinking fast. He saw Politician's submachine gun and had to know he didn't have a hope in hell of getting out alive.

He lunged at Lyons, the sharp blade glittering, and Blancanales let his weapon rip full throttle. Bits and pieces of the young assassin splattered the walls as he began a jerky dance of death. It seemed to take forever—two, three seconds, tops—and then the magazine was spent, the blade man toppling over backward with a breathless sigh.

Blancanales knelt in front of Lyons, checking out the damage, noting needle tracks along the inside of his arms. Before he had a chance to try to rouse Ironman, there were footsteps in the corridor behind him. Blancanales dug for his automatic, turning.

Schwarz and Turrin stood in the doorway, taking in the scene and looking stunned.

"Sweet Jesus!" Turrin rasped.

"Is he breathing?" Schwarz asked.

Blancanales turned back in time to catch a crooked, bloodstained smile from Lyons.

"Christ," Ironman whispered through his pain, "what kept you guys?"

5

Five minutes into his appointed vigil Eric Shanks began to wonder if he had a bull's-eye painted on his back. Each vehicle that crossed the nearby intersection seemed to slow a trifle more than necessary, hostile faces checking out the gringo as they passed. A motorcycle backfire nearly made him break for cover, but he stood his ground and forced a jaunty smile instead.

Across the street his cameraman was watching from a second-story window, taping every movement he made.

In case.

During the past few days, Shanks had observed enough of life in Medellín to know that everyone was vulnerable all the time. The night a number of his colleagues were machine-gunned in a local bar, dumb luck and heavy furniture had saved his life. No sooner had the People's Army of Colombia claimed credit for the massacre than Shanks was witness to the public murder of the nation's minister of justice. In between the two events police in Medellín kept right on chalking up the ten to fifteen daily murders everyone accepted as a normal fact of life.

It was enough to make a person paranoid, and Shanks was half convinced that someone, somewhere, had his name on a death list, ticking off the final hours of his life. In other circumstances he might well have pulled the plug, demanded reassignment, and to hell with any backlash from the network. He'd paid his dues and then some, from

Afghanistan to the mean streets in Miami and the nation's capital, and Shanks no longer felt a need to prove himself.

But he was angry now. Costanza and the rest of the cartel had pissed him off. He was determined not to leave Colombia without a story that would blow the narcobaron's socks off.

And so the urgent call had hooked him right away.

It made no difference that his cameraman and friend of seven years had instantly dismissed the summons as a trap. Shanks recognized the possibility, but he'd also witnessed the cartel in action, slaughtering their enemies in total disregard to innocent civilians or observers from the press. Costanza might demand his death and never miss a beat, but there would be no need to stage a rendezvous.

Besides, during the past few days in Medellín, someone was hitting back. The *narcotraficantes* had been suffering strategic losses of their own, endemic violence turning into something of a two-edged sword. It was a change of pace, to say the least—and not unwelcome in the eyes of many victims who had seen their families torn apart by random bombings, shoot-outs and abductions on the street.

Shanks had a sneaking hunch his nameless caller might be able to supply some answers in regard to the attacks upon Costanza and his chief competitors. No explanation for the backlash had been promised, but the lure was sweet enough to hook him.

The newsman would recall the graveyard voice until his dying day.

"I have a member of the People's Army under wraps. He wants to talk about Costanza and the journalists who were killed."

It was enough.

Shanks had presumed a link between Costanza's network and the PAC, but no one had uncovered any solid evidence to make the case. If he could bag a member of the rebel underground and put him on the air, expose the

Medellín cartel's complicity in killing American journalists...

Hell, he might be looking at a goddamn Pulitzer! If nothing else, the news would make Costanza sweat, and that was damn near good enough to justify the risk involved.

Shanks lit a cigarette and reviewed his options if the meet went wrong or blew up in his face. There was a restaurant behind him, less than thirty feet away, where he could try for cover in a pinch. The problem would be spotting his assailants before they mowed him down. That was why he had a camera rolling from the window just above a tailor's shop.

If he was marked to die this afternoon, at least his final moments would be ready for an airing nationwide at six o'clock.

He gave up counting cars, disgusted with the game, but still kept one eye on the street. As best he could, Shanks also scrutinized the shoppers and pedestrians around him, knowing that assassins could approach on foot, as well as in a car or riding on the pillion of a motorbike.

A silenced pistol or a blade between the ribs would do the job as well as any grandiose display of automatic weaponry.

He'd considered going armed, but Shanks was conscious of his limitations. He'd witnessed several dozen violent deaths and filmed the aftermath of several hundred more, but he wasn't a fighter. If it came down to playing Wyatt Earp, Shanks knew that he'd likely shoot himself or drop a harmless passerby before he bagged the enemy.

Instead, he had a different way of fighting. His weapons were the camera and the microphone, with popular opinion backing up his play. It had been years since Shanks believed he was winning hearts or minds, but he could sell a story with the best, and anyone who took him lightly was a fool.

He registered the van subconsciously, its gray bulk slowing through the intersection, edging to the curb a half block down. Shanks made no move to follow, staying where he was within the camera's line of sight. He flicked his cigarette away and faced the second-story window, praying that his backup hadn't chosen just this moment to relieve himself.

Downrange, a side door opened on the van. A slim Hispanic dressed in denim work clothes exited the vehicle and made a beeline back to the newsman.

Colombian?

The newsman frankly couldn't say.

"I've seen you on television."

It wasn't the caller's voice. Shanks frowned. "That's possible."

"You're waiting for a lift, I think."

"Nobody mentioned anything about a ride."

The stranger shrugged, half turning toward the van. "Your choice," he said. "You understand, we're not prepared to make delivery on the street like this."

He shot another glance across the street and felt the new arrival pick it up. Instead of taking off, he turned to face the hidden lens and flashed a winning smile. The gutsy bastard waved before he swiveled back toward Shanks. "We're done with *Candid Camera* now, all right? I haven't got all day."

Shanks gave himself a beat to think about it, finally nodded, then fell into step behind his escort as they backtracked to the waiting van.

MACK BOLAN RECOGNIZED the journalist at once, despite the nervous attitude that never showed up on TV. Encizo followed him inside the van and closed the sliding door.

"We had to stop and make a newsreel," he told Bolan. "Anyway, we're set."

Shanks found himself a place directly opposite the Executioner. Encizo took the shotgun seat, and Jack Grimaldi put the van in motion, cruising aimlessly and watching for a tail. On Bolan's left the lone survivor of their strike against the People's Army wore a gag and handcuffs, staring at his knees as if he'd never noticed them before.

"I think we need some introductions here," the newsman said.

"Names aren't important," Bolan said. "I've been following your broadcasts, Mr. Shanks."

"That's good to know." He allowed a hint of irony to mask his apprehension as he settled in and braced himself against the motion of the van.

"You covered the assassination."

"I was there." Shanks frowned, remembering. "I wouldn't say we had it covered."

"But you got the story out."

"I did my job."

"It's more than that."

"You think so?"

Bolan held the newsman's gaze. "I'm banking on it."

Shanks was first to look away. He focused on the rebel prisoner and asked, "Is this my story?"

"He's your confirmation," Bolan said. "The story is Luis Costanza using left-wing terrorists to carry out attacks on the media. American reporters massacred because they spread the word about Costanza and his playmates."

"You don't have to brief me on the shooting. I was there."

"It didn't scare you off."

"You want to know the truth? It *pissed* me off. If I was smart enough to stop and think about it, I suppose I'd catch the next flight home."

"I doubt that very much."

"You take a lot for granted—like me showing up to meet a total stranger in the middle of a war zone."

"Here you are."

"Touché. Suppose I say we've sparred enough. Can we get down to business?"

"Anytime."

"Let's try right now."

The warrior looked him over. "Are you wired?"

Shanks shook his head. "I hate those things. The last time out I had a short and damn near set myself on fire."

Encizo passed a compact tape recorder back to Bolan, and he switched it on. "The tape's yours when we're finished. Incidentally it's clean. No prints."

Shanks took a chance. "That wouldn't stop me picking out your faces."

The Executioner admired his nerve. "We won't be taking part in any lineups."

"Are you sure?"

"I'd bet my life."

"Okay, let's talk about Costanza."

And they did for close to forty minutes, Bolan running down the details of the raid that had resulted in the death of a half-dozen journalists. He linked the People's Army with the Medellín cartel through payoffs and delivery of weapons to the underground. Costanza's payback was an occasional demand for service in the form of an abduction, bombing or assassination. Such had been the case with M-19's assault upon the Palace of Justice in 1985. More recently the U.S. press corps had been targeted for its unflattering reportage of the *narcotraficantes* and their ruthless war against society at large.

Shanks nodded toward their muzzled passenger. "He'll back this up with the specifics?"

"All you need is an interpreter."

"No sweat. You want to tell me where you picked him up?"

By now the warrior knew their raid against the People's Army would be on the air, complete with body counts. He figured Eric Shanks would be the only newsman in the city unaware of what had happened to the rebel band.

"We hit the PAC this morning," Bolan answered, "just before I phoned you. He's all that's left."

Shanks stared at Bolan for a moment, went pale, then flushed cherry-red. "You wiped them out? In Medellín?"

"Relax. You're sitting on the day's exclusive. I suggest you make connections for a pickup when we let you off, and get your boy on video before you hand him over to the DAS."

"If this is all some kind of game—"

"I've got no stake in making you look foolish, Shanks. We share a common enemy. Your network is a weapon that can hit him in the ego, where he lives. With any luck a confirmation of Costanza's link with terrorism will help get the State Department off its fat collective ass."

"I take it you're from Justice?"

"Self-employed. The details have no bearing on your story."

"I'd prefer to be the judge of that."

"Not this time."

Shanks was on the verge of arguing, but he thought better of it. "I don't want to walk around the streets with him, like that."

"Your office building has a back door on the alley," Bolan told him. "We can drop you there. Nobody has to see you going in."

"I see you do your homework."

"It's the only way I know to stay ahead." Or stay alive, he thought, and kept it to himself.

"Okay, you're on."

Ten minutes put them in the alleyway behind a downtown office complex. Shanks sat tensely until a group of children passed by and disappeared around the corner. "Somebody's bound to ask me how I found this guy."

"So tell them everything you know," Bolan said. "It couldn't hurt."

"I'm not sure they'd believe it, anyway."

"You never know."

Encizo let him out and dragged the handcuffed rebel from the van. A moment later he was back and settled in the shotgun seat. Grimaldi put the vehicle in gear and took them out of there.

"You think he'll play it straight?" the Cuban asked.

The Executioner was focusing on empty space, already thinking several moves ahead, but he responded automatically. "I wouldn't be a bit surprised."

LUIS COSTANZA WAS sick to death of bad news pouring in from every side. The extradition of his second-in-command to the United States was bad enough, made that much worse by the unseating of Caseros and his friendly government in Panama. Costanza had attempted to recoup his losses with the execution of Benito Franco, thereby silencing a major voice of criticism in the national regime, but he had cause to wonder if the move had been a tactical mistake.

This morning over breakfast he'd been disturbed by the announcement of a paramilitary raid against the People's Army of Colombia, in Medellín. From all appearances the red commandos had been decimated in their urban hideout, taken by surprise and slaughtered by an enemy who had no interest in retrieving prisoners.

Or so it seemed until the television news came on at twelve o'clock.

Costanza soon discovered there had, indeed, been a survivor of the raid. He was in custody, protected by the government and speaking freely of the PAC's connection to the Medellín cartel. Worse yet, before he was incarcerated there had been a lengthy interview with Eric Shanks, a gringo journalist whose editorials had ridiculed Costanza for the past few weeks.

It was a shame, Costanza thought, that Shanks had managed to survive the shooting that had silenced several of his friends a few days earlier. Next time perhaps.

But meanwhile the disclosure of a positive connection with the revolutionary left could only harm Costanza, further tarnishing his reputation in the halls of congress and among the right-wing businessmen who winked at his involvement in the drug trade, cheerfully accepting his contention that cocaine was critical to the Colombian economy.

Such men had helped support Costanza when he hired the
two Israelis, Auerbach and Feldman, to instruct their rank-
and-file employees in effective methods of defense against
the rebel scum. It made Costanza seem a hypocrite—or
worse—to deal with both sides equally when many of his
close associates believed the future of their nation was en-
dangered by the People's Army and affiliated groups.

If there was one thing Costanza valued over cold, hard
cash, it was his reputation as a patriot and a philanthro-
pist. He couldn't stand by idly while his name was linked
with anarchists and radicals. It undermined the very es-
sence of his manufactured image, jeopardizing all he'd
worked for in the past two decades.

Such slander called for some response, but he couldn't
afford to face his enemies in one-on-one debate. The late
Benito Franco had embarrassed him in public once, and it
would be some time before Costanza risked another drub-
bing in the presence of an audience.

Instead, he thought in terms of silencing his critics, wiping out his opposition at the source.

One step had been completed prior to Franco's death,
with restoration of the peace between himself and his
preeminent competitors, Rodriguez and Mercado. It was
doubtful they could coexist for long, but even days might be
enough to see him through the present crisis. Afterward,
there'd be time enough to deal with any loose ends dangling
in the breeze.

His first step, painful as it was, would have to be Ortega.
Surrounded by persuasive agents of the DEA and the FBI,
it would require a man of steel to hold his tongue and risk a
hundred years in prison when he could release himself by
telling tales. Ortega was a battle-hardened comrade who had
proved himself repeatedly, but he was also made of flesh and
blood. It stood to reason that his own self-interest would
prevail in times of trial.

It was a simple fact of life—and death.

Costanza listened to the hollow sound of the long-distance line, his index finger tapping out the numbers to connect him with Maria Teresina at her safehouse in the Everglades. Regardless of the trouble she was facing on her own, he trusted the woman to perform on cue. If anyone could reach Ortega in his federal cell, Costanza's killer would find a way.

The telephone rang twice before a small, recorded voice informed Costanza that completion of his call would be impossible. He tried twice more, with an identical result, before he punched up a second number from memory.

This time the call was answered by a human being. Passwords were exchanged before Costanza asked to speak with La Araña or her second-in-command. His knuckles whitened, fingers welded to the telephone with sudden perspiration as he listened to the curt reply. Costanza's head was swimming as he cradled the receiver, sinking back into his leather chair.

Another grievous blow, as if he hadn't suffered quite enough already. Somehow, someone had succeeded in uprooting his Miami operation, leaving it in total disarray. Maria Teresina and a number of her soldiers were dead, the small-fry competition flocking in from every side to steal her customers before Costanza could recuperate.

He'd be forced to start from scratch in Florida. It wouldn't be easy, but it could be done.

Before he tackled that dilemma, though, Costanza had to make his own home base secure against attack. That meant identifying his elusive enemies and running them to earth, destroying each and every one as an example.

So much to do; so little time.

Costanza wiped his palm against the fabric of his custom-tailored slacks and reached out for the telephone again. A local call this time.

He needed help, and it was time for Isaac Auerbach to earn his daily bread.

"THAT'S IT. Like that."

The woman smiled, redoubling her efforts. It was difficult to answer with her mouth full, and she didn't try.

Reclining naked in an easy chair, his one eye closed, the muscular Israeli set his mind adrift. The woman knelt beside him, working, and he left her to it, reaching out to stroke her raven hair with one hand as he might reward a favored pet for some small gesture of obedience.

In fact, he'd paid more for purebred hunting dogs than he'd pay the whore this afternoon, but he was pleased with her performance all the same. She had a firm, young body and a pleasant face. Above all else she took direction beautifully.

He felt the pressure mounting in his groin and quickly tangled fingers in her hair to pull her mouth away. "Not yet."

She moved in close enough for him to cup her breast, the large hand gliding lower, fingers rummaging between her thighs. He wasn't gentle, but the woman was accustomed to rough handling, and the one-eyed gringo didn't cause her pain deliberately. He simply lacked finesse.

A small deficiency for which he compensated her in cash.

When the internal blaze had faded to a pleasant glow, he put her back to work.

The telephone distracted him. He reached it with his left hand, never stirring from his chair. The woman glanced up briefly from her labor, but he gave no signal to desist, so she went back to work.

"Hello."

"Are you alone?"

He recognized Costanza's voice at once, a portion of his mind alert and ready to respond. "Not quite."

"I need you. Bring our friend along."

"How soon?"

"Within the hour."

"Affirmative."

As he replaced the handset, Isaac Auerbach experienced a tingle of excitement that was wholly independent of the warm lips working in his lap. Distinct and separate feelings, each one primal and compelling in its way—his sex drive, and the thrill of combat once removed.

If he was forced to choose, the trim Israeli knew exactly which one he'd pick. Unlike the female of the species, blood and death had never let him down.

"I have a job to do," he said. "Please finish now."

The woman brought her warm hands into play, and Auerbach deliberately made his mind a blank, forgetting all about Costanza and the need for tracking Feldman down before they met. It scarcely mattered what the narcobaron wanted them to do. They were employed to follow orders and obtain desired results.

A heartbeat prior to climax, it occurred to Auerbach that he was bought and paid for, not unlike the woman kneeling by his chair. The crucial difference was that he enjoyed his work, and Auerbach was not dependent on the whimsy of his clientele.

6

Brognola recognized the trilling of his private line without a glance in the direction of the dual telephones to check for winking lights. He scooped it up before the soft sound could be repeated.

"Yes?"

The distant voice of Barbara Price came back at him from Stony Man Farm. "We just heard from Miami, Hal."

"I'm listening." The butterflies inside his stomach felt more like a swarm of killer bees.

"We've got that missing package back," she told him, sounding pleased.

"Condition."

"Could be worse. We're waiting on a damage estimate right now."

Brognola let himself relax a bit, surrendering to sweet relief at hearing Lyons was alive. Not well, exactly—that would be too much to hope for given the circumstances—but Barbara would have found a way to tip him off if it was anything irreparable.

"The rest of it?"

"I spoke with the exterminators. They assured me your spider problems in the house down there are history."

"Clean sweep?"

"The next best thing."

"No further complications?"

"Well, there *was* a minor problem on the legal end."

"Explain."

"The opposition's counsel caught a bug before they had a chance to meet him. I'm afraid it's done him in."

Brognola pictured Alexander Constantine and found himself devoid of sympathy. "Tough break."

"No word from farther south as yet." There was a wistfulness in Barbara's tone that echoed in Brognola's soul.

"We have to keep our fingers crossed," he said. "At least the odds look better now with Phoenix on the team."

"It's still a lousy bet."

"We knew that going in. Why don't you get some rest?"

"I will," she promised, neither one of them believing it. "And I'll get back to you as soon as we hear anything about Ironman."

"Day or night," Brognola said.

"You got it, Chief."

On balance it appeared that things were going reasonably well. With Lyons safe and La Araña dead, they had a glimpse of something close to victory in southern Florida. Costanza would require some time to mend his fences in the Sunshine State, and if the troops in Medellín were up to snuff, the dealer would discover that he had his hands full in his own backyard.

Brognola knew they weren't about to win the war on drugs in Florida, much less Colombia, but that didn't preclude the good guys picking up a solid local score, for once. From the big Fed's view the removal of a leech like Alexander Constantine was icing on the cake, but Barbara Price might take it differently.

He sat back and spent a moment pondering the information he'd gleaned from their discussion. Constantine apparently had been the subject of surveillance by Costanza's team, and something had alerted the cartel to his potential status as a liability. From that point it would be a natural development for Costanza to cut his losses, passing orders to Maria Teresina for a hit.

Eliminating Constantine could well have been the woman's final task before she went to her reward.

Brognola wondered briefly whether La Araña had been able to obtain substantial information from Carl Lyons in the four days he was missing. Each and every member of Brognola's team was specially trained in methods of resisting physical interrogation, up to and including sessions of hypnosis to provide a partial antidote for the effects of certain chemicals. Despite all that he knew every man was breakable, provided the inquisitors had proper tools and ample time.

If Carl had broken, spilling even part of what he knew, Costanza would possess one more advantage in a war where all the odds were in his favor from the start. If he could finger Bolan or Grimaldi, any member of the Phoenix team...

Brognola closed his mind to the depressing implications. They'd faced the possibility of leaks before—with Stony Man itself besieged by enemies on one occasion—and they'd endured, absorbed their losses, grieved in private and continued pressing hard against the common foe.

But past tense didn't mean a thing.

Each battle was a brand-new situation, fraught with possibilities and peril. Every time his soldiers took the field their lives were on the line.

And Hal Brognola sweated out the darkest hours with them every time.

Like now.

The fact that he'd gone out on a limb without authority was hardly worth considering at this point in the game. His own career had been a full one—too damn full, according to a number of his critics on the Hill—and if they booted him tomorrow, he'd still survive.

Brognola couldn't say the same for his combatants in the field.

It came down to a test of strength and wills beyond the abstract terms of good and evil, right and wrong. Brognola had observed enough of grim reality to know that crime *did* pay, and that the good guys didn't always win. Sometimes the black hats walked away with all the marbles, and the cavalry was too damn late to save the day.

Some days there simply wasn't anything to save.

If it were up to fate, then nothing Hal Brognola said or did would make a bit of difference in the end. Conversely if the outcome hung on guts and sheer determination, he was betting everything he had on Bolan and the Phoenix team.

They were the best.

Brognola only hoped they were good enough.

SOMETIMES IT DIDN'T HELP to know you were in the right.

The quick round-trip to Florida had been an impulse, something Barbara Price had felt she owed herself and every other member of the Phoenix team. Confronting Alexander Constantine was better than a helping hand to comrades on the firing line; it was a chance to stretch her wings and see what she could do away from Stony Man without the network of computers and communications gear to back her up.

So far so good.

She went in fully armed with information from the Justice files, and Constantine had folded like a soggy house of cards. For Barbara it had been enough to see him crumble, knowing he was out of it before Ortega and Caseros hit Miami, kicking off a series of appeals that might drag on for years.

It was enough for her to see the lawyer run. She didn't need to see him locked away, much less exterminated.

Something had gone wrong, and she'd have to live with that.

A search of the *Hung Jury* had revealed sophisticated listening devices, after which the searchers turned up more in Constantine's apartment and his business office, even the cellular phone in his custom Mercedes. The guy was covered any way he turned, but it had taken several hours to determine *who* was watching him—or, rather, who wasn't.

The DEA officially denied participation, as did spokesmen for the FBI, the IRS and Metro-Dade. No orders for the bugging were on file with either state or federal courts in southern Florida, which mean they were illegal and the evidence obtained from listening to Constantine and company wouldn't have been admissible in court. To Barbara's mind that didn't rule out an official presence in the case—investigators had been known to lie about their bugs from time to time—but since the lawyer's death, she had another suspect fixed in mind.

Costanza.

There would be no better way to keep an eye on his attorney in the States, and any narcobaron worth his salt could pay for the arrangements out of pocket change. Costanza or his stooges had been listening to every phone call, every conversation Constantine engaged in at his office, at his home or on his yacht. They must have known enough about his appetites and sex life to produce a juicy kiss-and-tell, but they'd missed their chance.

One conversation in particular had sealed the lawyer's fate. When Barbara Price confronted Constantine that afternoon, revealing evidence that could have booked him an exclusive federal lockup for the next ten years or so, he folded, going back on his commitment to defend Costanza's number two in the United States. He'd been unconscious of the secret ears around him as he laid his plans to slip away, escape Costanza's reach and find himself a place to hide until it all blew over, maybe years from now.

Of course, Costanza had been with him all the way, his people waiting on the yacht or close behind their quarry when he boarded. They'd mutilated Constantine and left him as an example to the next man who was brave enough—or scared enough—to try to buck the Medellín cartel.

Beneath it all a single thought kept gnawing at the core of Barbara's mind.

I killed him.

It wasn't as if she'd walked up to Constantine and pulled out a gun. Oh, no, that would have been more merciful, the way it all came down. And she'd shared the lawyer's ignorance of microphones concealed around his office when they had their little chat.

But ignorance was no excuse. Her action prompted Constantine to run, and flight had killed him.

If Barbara had ignored the mouthpiece in Miami, he'd almost certainly have done his bit in court for both Esteban Ortega and the toppled president of Panama, Hector Caseros. It was doubtful whether he could rescue either client from a one-way cruise along Shit Creek, but Constantine was—had been—clever, even brilliant in a sleazy sort of way.

When all was said and done, the fact remained that Barbara *did* confront the lawyer in his office, hidden bugs and all. Costanza *had* been listening, and Constantine *did* try to run.

Case closed; next case.

It shouldn't feel like this, she told herself. How many times had her directives led to death and suffering in the recent past? The men she supervised weren't out there playing hopscotch with the enemy—they were eliminating lethal predators to save the larger flock.

Miami's Alexander Constantine had ranked among the predators, and it was pure coincidence that some of his associates had finished him before he kept a dead-end date with Able Team. Would she have felt this way if Schwarz or Blancanales had reported killing Constantine?

No way.

Because it wouldn't be my fault.

"I need a break," she said.

"You've earned it," Aaron Kurtzman answered, swiveling his chair to face her as she rose. "Take all you need. I'll buzz you if we catch a hot one."

"Thanks. I owe you one."

"I'm looking forward to it."

"Sexist oinker."

"Oh, so true."

Undressing for the steamy shower that she craved, Price finally admitted to herself that she had other worries on her mind beyond the fate of Alexander Constantine. If she had more blood on her hands, it was a simple matter of degree—a variation in her personal involvement with the war she helped support from her position safe behind the lines.

The root of her anxiety, she realized, had less to do with Constantine than the combatants in her charge who were—at least presumably—still fighting for their lives in Florida and Medellín.

The worst of it was over in Miami, she decided. Lyons would be laid up for a while, but the prognosis seemed to indicate no crippling injuries. His partners in the blitz had all emerged unscathed, other than a few brand-new worry lines and a few gray hairs that bespoke their anxiety since Lyons's disappearance. The relatively minor damage balanced out against destruction of Costanza's strong right arm in Florida, a major body blow against the Medellín cartel.

In Panama the men of Phoenix Force had staged a brilliant coup against Caseros, managing to frustrate his escape and bring him into custody when Operation Just Cause toppled his eccentric government. No telling how their case would wind up in a federal courtroom, but the demagogue was out of office now without a realistic hope of a comeback.

Which left Medellín.

Costanza might be shaken, even wounded, but he wasn't down and out. His recent murder of the nation's highest-ranking lawman was an indication of the man's arrogance and power. He was used to crushing opposition with a ruthlessness that left survivors in no doubt of who was boss. For years the government in Bogotá had managed to ignore Costanza's reign of terror, getting by with weak denunciations in the press and a few low-level raids to justify the salaries drawn by the police.

It would require a miracle, she thought, to root out Costanza and punish him for his innumerable crimes. She wondered whether Bolan and the others had a chance in hell to walk away from Medellín, much less succeed in their attempt at breaking the cartel.

The shower's heat enveloped Price, and she tried to make her mind a blank, expelling thoughts of narcopolitics and sudden death. Ten minutes stolen for herself would make no difference in the grander scheme of things. A lonely woman bathing in the Blue Ridge Mountains of Virginia wouldn't make a ripple in the boiling caldron of Colombia.

And loneliness was part of it, she realized, defeated in her bid to push anxiety aside. She missed Mack Bolan, even though they rarely saw each other, no more than three or four times a year. Short hours at a time, a day or two at most. Their private interludes were sandwiched into stolen moments after briefings, in between the Executioner's arrival and departure for the latest battleground.

It seemed ridiculous the more she thought about it. Given the circumstances, it was difficult even to claim a viable relationship, much less a "love affair." And when she put her feelings underneath a microscope, she was immediately taken by the absence of romantic sentiment where Bolan was concerned—no dreams of a secluded cottage with a picket fence and ivy climbing on the walls; no children in the yard or yapping dogs to send the mailman on his way.

In fact, if someone had demanded a concise and tidy definition of her feelings, Barbara would have been struck dumb. She loved Mack Bolan, in her way, but they weren't *in* love. Their intersecting lives made no allowances for dreams or simple privacy. She asked for and expected nothing but the chance to do her job.

And yet the thought of Bolan lying in a ditch somewhere—or stretched out on a grimy sidewalk covered by a sheet—brought sudden tears to Barbara's eyes.

Damn fool.

She turned and raised her face beneath the shower, feeling grateful as the water washed her angry tears away.

IT WAS THE WORST TIME of the day to fly, but Leo Turrin had already seen enough of southern Florida to last a lifetime. Pacing off the crowded concourse at Miami International, he was relieved that Gadgets and Politician had remained behind to baby-sit Lyons at the hospital.

Their part of it was over, but he had to give them credit for endurance. Halfway back, along Tamiami Trail, the gutsy men had been making plans to catch a flight for Medellín that afternoon as soon as Carl was safely stashed away and under guard.

Brognola's veto scuttled that idea, reminding them that Bolan had Grimaldi and Phoenix Force on-site already, not to mention a contingent from the Great White North. More gringos on the street would only jeopardize the play, and it had cut no ice when Blancanales claimed he could pass for local color in a pinch.

For Turrin's part, he was surprised to find himself anticipating the return to Wonderland as something of a sweet relief. For all its crime and squalor, street gangs and the scent of unadulterated bullshit wafting from the Hill, he'd be going home to Angelina and a life where people—most of them at least—returned from casual dates without a four-day search and a blazing firefight tacked onto the schedule of events.

There was a time when he'd taken violent death for granted, as an everyday occurrence in his world, but Turrin's frontline days were well behind him. The tour with Schwarz and Blancanales had been something of a shock, reminding him of the distance he'd traveled from his service as an undercover agent in the East Coast Mafia. It wasn't that he missed those days exactly, but he wondered sometimes whether Bolan and the rest experienced a different quality of life, compelled to savor every moment of the day as if it were their last.

No point in looking back, he thought. A man made choices in his life, then lived with those decisions. Or sometimes he took them to an early grave.

Twenty minutes remained until his flight was called for boarding. Turrin found a seat and settled in to wait, immediately sorry he hadn't paused to buy a magazine or a paperback when there was time. It would have helped distract him from the thoughts of Medellín, and other lives at risk.

Fat chance.

Within the next half hour he'd be returning home to Washington, but part of him was drifting southward even now. A prayer perhaps for other soldiers caught up in a storm that had to run its course for good or ill.

The man from Justice closed his eyes and wondered which of them would have the grit required to stand before that killer wind.

AT HALF PAST ONE in Medellín Mack Bolan huddled in a temporary safehouse with Grimaldi and the men of Phoenix Force. A new addition to the team was Sergeant Charlie McPherson working undercover for the Royal Canadian Mounted Police. Three other Mounties had the watch outside, protecting the assemblage from a rude surprise.

"Your buddy Shanks is making quite a splash," Jack Grimaldi said. "Every daily in the States'll pick up bits and pieces of his story for tomorrow's morning run. If they don't feel heat from *that* in Washington, we're wasting time."

"It's not about publicity or turning up the heat on Congress," Bolan replied. "We've got enough laws on the books already, but they haven't turned the tide."

"You think we will?" Calvin James asked.

"I *know* you did in Panama. We're bound to try in Medellín."

"Too bad about Costanza's reconciliation with Rodriguez and Mercado," Katz said.

"We still might have an angle there. They talk like allies, but they still don't trust each other where it counts. I wouldn't be surprised to see Costanza set his 'good friends' up as stalking-horses if he thinks it'll help."

"Or maybe we could make them *think* he's done as much," McCarter added, looking none the worse for wear since his interrogation by the Panamanian authorities.

"It's worth a look," Bolan allowed.

"Is anybody earmarked for the Justice spot?" Gary Manning asked.

Turning from the window as he spoke, McPherson fielded that one on his own. "I spoke to Bogotá this morning. Considering the relative longevity of recent justice ministers, it comes as no surprise that they've run short of candidates. The job goes begging—for the moment, anyway."

"Another point for the Costanza team," Manning grumbled.

"Costanza's operating on the edge," Bolan said, hoping it was true. "We know he's pulled back to his hardsite on the Río Nechi, north of town. He's lost Órtega and a seat in congress, his connection with the PAC, the best part of his network in Miami. Any way you run it down, the past week has to be his worst in years."

Across the room Katz frowned and cleared his throat. "The point is, will he be around *next* week?"

"We've only got two options left that I can see," Bolan told them. "Either draw him out of hiding or go in and hit him where he lives."

"What happened to the easy part?" Grimaldi joked.

"The easy part was getting here," McCarter answered him. "The hard part's getting home again."

"I'm glad you mentioned that. I was afraid we had a chance there for a second."

Bolan let the banter run its course, aware that each and every one of them was tense from seven days of full-time action on the firing line. Phoenix Force had worked a minor miracle in Panama with the Caseros coup, and they were still prepared to go the distance with Costanza in Colombia.

They were the best.

"So what's the plan?" Grimaldi asked.

"I'd like to stir the pot some more," Bolan replied. "Shake up Mercado and Rodriguez a little bit and let their built-in paranoia run from there. Costanza thinks he's patched things up enough to make it work. We need to show him he's wrong."

"My men and I would like to help in any way we can," McPherson told the room at large. "I know we're strangers to your operation, but we've got a stake in what goes on here, all the same. Costanza and his bunch of vermin have been spreading misery across the map up north from Vancouver to Halifax."

"I've got no problem with a helping hand," the Executioner replied. "You might have noticed that we're not exactly playing by the rules."

"What rules are those?" McPherson asked. "You mean the one that lets a dealer walk away with fines or ninety days in jail for poisoning a child? I've had the rules, and then some. We're a bit outside our lawful jurisdiction as it is."

The Mountie seemed sincere enough, but Bolan wouldn't let him off the hook. Not yet.

"The extradition on Ortega was a fluke," he said. "From this point on we take no prisoners."

"Suits me," McPherson answered, standing as solid as a rock while seven pairs of eyes bored into him. "As far as I'm concerned, a trial's a waste of honest money for the likes of these."

"Your people feel the same?"

"Let's say they volunteered to do a job. So far they haven't had a chance to break a sweat."

A glance around the room found Jack Grimaldi and the Phoenix warriors nodding, one by one. A silent affirmation of new entries in the game of life and death.

"Okay," Bolan said finally. "I've got a few ideas for turning up the heat. Jump in with anything you think might help. Here's what we do...."

7

Chaim Feldman nosed the sleek Mercedes into traffic, circling once around the block and checking his rearview mirror to be sure they hadn't picked up a tail. Beside him Isaac Auerbach was silent, apparently distracted by the summons that had put them on the road.

"He's pissed about the PAC, I guess?"

"He wasn't pleased."

"And we're supposed to make it right."

"That's what we're paid for."

Feldman carefully avoided showing any sign of his dissatisfaction with the deal. It had been sweet enough until the past few days. A healthy paycheck, as regular as clockwork, and their major task had been conducting seminars for gunmen hired by right-wing farmers and the rulers of the Medellín cartel. Ostensibly they were preparing local patriots to hold their own against guerrillas, Communists and cattle thieves. In fact, it came as no surprise to anyone when graduates of their intensive courses turned up on the back of motorcycles, spraying automatic gunfire at this or that selected enemy of the Costanza syndicate.

A rugged pragmatist, Chaim Feldman had no qualms about participating in the education of assassins. It was all a matter of degree, in politics and business. When the players had sufficient money on the line, they found a way to shore up those investments and protect themselves against attack.

The rich made enemies and lived in fear.

It was a simple fact of life.

The answer, for selected clients, was Trans-Global Security Consultants, the firm pioneered by Auerbach and Feldman following their separation from the Mossad. Between them they had precious years invested in the art of violent death, and those who qualified to dish it out were likewise able to advise potential targets on the prospects for avoiding same.

Who better to instruct a team of bodyguards than two professional assassins who had served their country long and well by slipping past the guard of Arab terrorists and surgically removing leaders from Fatah, Jihad and Black September? Auerbach and Feldman were adept at spotting loopholes in a client's armor—or advising him how to take advantage of another's weaknesses.

It was a living, and a decent one at that.

Until last week.

Before the Panamanian debacle they'd managed to refine their schedule so the training camps had nearly run themselves. A handful of Colombians had been selected as instructors, trained to a degree where they could function in the absence of their superiors...but not enough to make the two Israelis seem expendable. A brief trip out of the country to relax had seemed no problem at the time.

And then all hell had broken loose.

Their largest training camp had been attacked—demolished, really—by assailants who remained anonymous, effectively beyond their reach. Throughout the province violent clashes left Costanza's operation reeling, while his chief competitors faced savage opposition of their own.

It was the first hint of the coming storm.

That storm had broken over Panama a few days later, catching Auerbach and Feldman in a sanctuary that had suddenly become a trap. Almost before they knew it U.S. troops were dropping from the skies and President Caseros was himself a prisoner. The summons from Costanza, drawing Auerbach and Feldman back to Medellín, had been a godsend, but it nearly came too late.

There had been trouble waiting for them at the airport, in the form of loose surveillance by a stranger neither one of them had recognized. Their rolling backup saved the day, disabling the tracker's wheels in a convenient "accident," without the gunplay that would certainly have made their reappearance in Colombia a federal case.

The stranger's face had haunted Feldman ever since. He was a dark man, large and obviously competent, although they'd been able to deceive him once.

Feldman feared they might not have a second chance.

The public murder of Benito Franco had been carried off without prior consultation from Costanza. It had been a foolish move from Feldman's point of view—too much resultant heat—but the Israeli made a point of keeping unsolicited opinions to himself. A client of Costanza's sort was unpredictable, impulsive, and it made no sense at all to anger an immensely wealthy killer on his own turf.

"I like the Med this time of year," he told his partner, keeping it lighthearted as he drove.

"Let's find out what he wants before we start to pack."

"Of course."

A hint of reassurance, even so. He knew Auerbach was fond enough of living to protect himself, and if survival called for bailing out, well, they'd taught Costanza's army well enough that he should have no problem fending for himself. Desertion under fire would definitely rule out future clients in Colombia, but Feldman had seen quite enough of Bogotá and Medellín.

And if they stayed? Feldman trusted in his own ability, and Auerbach was legendary for his skill. They were survivors, with scars that testified to their endurance when the chips were down.

If nothing else, he'd prefer to know the number of his enemies, perhaps their names. It made a difference, stripping off the veil of mystery to humanize the opposition, thus investing them with common traits and weaknesses.

It made them easier to kill.

But easy never paid as well, another fact of life that Feldman recognized. Trans-Global drew the six- and seven-figure paychecks based upon their reputation for performing minor miracles—protecting men whose enemies were legion, penetrating the defenses of a rival who "couldn't be killed." They had a reputation to protect, not only in Colombia, but all around the world.

Which meant, of course, that they'd stay and fight . . . at least, until the cause was clearly lost.

From that point it was each man for himself, and let the devil take the slowest off the mark. Survival of the fittest was the one commandment that Feldman actively revered.

He'd survived this long by knowing when to kill, and when to quit.

But he'd hear Costanza out, discuss the odds with Auerbach and then decide. If he was forced to cut and run, another million-dollar payoff would allow his ego to recuperate in style.

Besides, it couldn't hurt to listen.

Not unless it got him killed.

LUIS COSTANZA WAITED, killing time until the Israelis arrived. To occupy his mind he left the house, strolling east along a flagstone path to reach his private zoo. Behind him native bodyguards with automatic rifles slung across their shoulders followed at a distance, trying to be inconspicuous.

The zoo had started as a whim, but men who take in several million dollars every day, year-round, are prone to make their whims reality. It covered nearly thirty acres of Costanza's property, complete with cages, pits and artificial habitats designed by experts in the field. Costanza's captive animals received more individual attention from their keepers than inhabitants of any major zoo in the United

States or Western Europe. They were fed on time, their living quarters cleaned with loving care, and any symptoms of illness or injury were reported to a special veterinarian in Medellín.

Costanza loved his animals, and if the members of his staff were sometimes less enchanted, they knew enough to treat the creatures with respect. Some of them still remembered Julio, and all had heard the story of the youth accused of baiting Costanza's matched pair of Bengal tigers, jabbing them with poles or cattle prods at feeding time. A hidden camera caught him at it, midway through his second week on the Costanza spread, and he was beaten bloody by the guards, stripped naked, then delivered to the tigers as their evening meal. Officially he was a "runaway," address unknown.

Costanza viewed the incident as an instructive lesson in priorities. Put simply, servants who abused their master's property didn't deserve to live.

He felt the same about his enemies and competitors in the business world. At some objective level of his mind, Costanza realized he wasn't ordained by God to dominate the traffic in cocaine, but he believed in an aggressive posture toward competitors. If they couldn't defend themselves with skill enough to win an enemy's respect—or cut a timely deal to save themselves—the world was better off without them. In a business where survivors made the rules up as they went along, Costanza was a master of the game.

But this time he was worried by the sheer persistence of his enemies, the way they melted into nothing when he tried to grab them by the throat. It galled him.

The murder of Benito Franco was a product of Costanza's anger and frustration in the past few days. It had been ill-advised perhaps, but it wasn't the first time dealers had removed a politician prior to expiration of his lawful term. Costanza had no interest in the angry, empty threats from Bogotá. His problems had their roots in Medellín, and they were growing by the day.

Destruction of the People's Army was a minor irritation to Costanza, but the seeming ease with which it was accomplished bothered him. Two dozen armed guerrillas massacred, apparently without a single injury among the raiders. Worse, the DAS and national police weren't responsible, a fact determined by Costanza's spies inside each group and their decided lack of crowing in the press. Four different right-wing groups took credit for the raid by lunchtime, but Costanza knew them all and saw through their transparent boasting at a glance.

The eradication of his rebel allies, minus one who turned up spilling everything he knew on television, had apparently been executed by the same anonymous combatants who had trashed Costanza's airstrip and the training camp for assassins. Undoubtedly the same men were responsible for the attacks on Rodriguez and Mercado. Picking out apparent links between the incidents was child's play, given twenty-twenty hindsight, but it didn't help Costanza to identify his enemies.

Gut instinct told him they'd be Americans—or hired by the Americans, at any rate. From that point on his logical deductions fell apart. It seemed unlikely that the White House would provoke a shooting war by murdering Colombians at home, but, then again, the military thrust in Panama had taken him completely by surprise.

If it wasn't the U.S. government, Costanza faced a range of possibilities including stateside mafiosi, Asians, Cubans and fanatic vigilantes—possibly a crackpot millionaire recruiting mercenaries for a private "war on drugs." Considering the options made his head hurt, and he put them out of mind, concentrating on his animals as he approached the zoo.

Costanza loved them all in different ways, but he was most enamored of the hunting cats. Their independence and ferocity appealed to him, reflecting qualities he valued in himself. They killed to live and showed no mercy to their prey, but it was nothing personal. He thought the world at large could take a lesson from the cats, and it had been Costanza's pleasure to instruct his staff when Julio abused his sacred privilege of observing them firsthand.

He dawdled past the tiger pit and the enclosure specially constructed for his mated pair of leopards. A pride of lions occupied the acreage next door, the bearded male and his four concubines relaxing underneath a shade tree, dozing in the midday heat. The jaguars watched Costanza with a grim intensity that made him smile, two hunters measuring their keeper for a meal.

He moved among the zebras, goats and antelopes from Africa, the strutting ostriches. Costanza always finished with the reptile house, hypnotically attracted to the snakes he'd collected from around the world. Emerging from the serpentarium, Costanza felt a subtle tremor in the earth beneath his feet. He turned to face the nearby mountains, picking out the profile of the live volcano standing like a sentry on the northern boundary of his land.

For some the close proximity of a volcano might have proved inhibiting where the construction of a multimillion-dollar palace was concerned. Luis Costanza viewed it in a different light, preferring to accept the challenge posed by Mother Earth. A brave man stood his ground, regardless of the danger, bending nature and his fellow man to serve his needs.

Costanza lived in the volcano's shadow for the same reason he murdered his enemies, or kept tigers and cobras a few hundred yards from his home. It helped define his status as a man of courage, one deserving of respect. While some men ran for cover when it rained, Costanza slept each night with the impending threat of fiery death.

He frowned and checked his watch, then started back in the direction of the house. Five minutes remained until the Israelis arrived, and there were preparations to be made. If there was one thing he could count on, it was Auerbach's punctuality.

The bodyguards fell into step behind him, shadows stretching out in front of them as they retreated from the sun.

THEY WERE EXPECTED, and the sentries on the gate waved Feldman through without a second glance. Auerbach automatically took note of numbers and deployment, weapons on display, the second line of troops held in reserve. Costanza's troops lacked military bearing, but they made up the deficiency in killer instinct and their willingness to learn.

Beyond the gate they drove for half a mile along the tree-lined drive, beside a man-made lake that had been stocked with game fish to amuse Costanza and his guests. Two hundred yards in length and half as wide, the lake had water piped from underground in season, if the rains fell short of popular demand. Along the banks imported reeds and grasses fostered the illusion of a reservoir carved out by nature's hand.

The house was vast, eighty rooms or more, but Auerbach wasn't impressed by the display of wealth, per se. If there was anything about Costanza he admired—or envied—it would have to be the narcobaron's power over other men. Investments were a transient thing—stock prices rose and fell; the stylish clothes and cars passed out of style; maintaining the most lavish home became monotonous in time—but power put a man on top and kept him there. It didn't matter if you slept beneath the desert sky or in a New York penthouse, if you dealt from strength—and most especially the power over life and death—you were a man to reckon with.

They parked around in back, and Feldman left the keys in the ignition. If there was a safe place to park the forty-thousand-dollar car in all Colombia, it would be outside Luis Costanza's home.

He vaguely recognized the man who met them on the porch. It would have been Ortega's job to see them in, but Auerbach had been informed of the arrest and extradition

order shortly after he returned from Panama. The hounds
were definitely yapping at Costanza's heels, but he was far
from down and out.

Inside, the lavish trappings were familiar—hand-carved
furniture, antiques and inlaid gold, elaborate tapestries on
several walls, the spotless carpeting that alternated here and
there with hardwood and parquet. Familiar with the general
layout of the floor plan, Auerbach had never taken time to
memorize it for himself. Costanza's home defense was left
to other hands.

The dealer's book-lined study was equivalent in size to
many midpriced condominiums. The desk was large enough
for Ping-Pong, and the shaded lamp was Tiffany. Costanza
moved to greet them as they entered, backlit by a wall of
glass that overlooked his gardens and the zoo beyond. They
shook hands all around, with Auerbach wondering if anyone had ever cracked the gilt-edged volumes filling the floor-
to-ceiling shelves.

"A glass of whiskey?"

Auerbach provided the correct response. "No, thank
you."

"Straight to business, then. Be seated, please."

They settled into heavy wood-and-leather chairs across
the desk from their employer.

"You're aware of what took place this morning in the
city?"

"With the People's Army? Yes."

"I'm convinced of a connection with other incidents."

"A logical assumption in the circumstances. Most especially since a member of the PAC has turned up in the
media."

Costanza frowned across the steeple of his fingers, meeting Auerbach's level gaze. "It's essential that we trace the
men responsible and punish them, whoever they may be. I
have a reputation to protect in Medellín, throughout Colombia. Such insults are impossible to tolerate."

"I understand."

In fact, he knew that ego barely scratched the surface of Costanza's flap. A multibillion-dollar empire was at stake, its ruler being kicked around by unknown strangers in his own backyard. If the attacks continued, small-fry from around the country and around the world would soon imagine they could do the same and walk away unscathed.

"There's a way," Costanza said. "I'm convinced we can smoke them out."

"Go on."

"You disagreed with me about eliminating Franco, Isaac."

"I expressed concern about the repercussions. It's too early to decide which one of us was right."

"And yet I have a way to use his death right now to our advantage."

"Oh?"

"He left a widow and a child. A daughter."

"Yes, I know the members of his family."

"If our enemies have some connection with the government—in Bogotá or otherwise—a pair of hostages would move them to negotiate, I think."

"And if they don't?"

"The same. With Franco's widow and the child in our protective custody, the DAS might be convinced to scour the countryside until our opposition is exposed and finally destroyed."

"Why not instruct your men to that effect right now? You have at least a quarter of the force on payroll, as it is."

"There have been certain difficulties. Failures of communication in the past few days."

"Since Franco's death?"

"The cause is immaterial."

"Of course."

"I want the woman and her child securely under lock and key tonight. Your job is to deliver them. I'll conduct the requisite negotiations on my own."

"You have the necessary information on her where-abouts and movements?"

"Everything you need shall be provided."

"It might be necessary to eliminate her bodyguards."

"As you think best."

"They would be DAS, perhaps F-2."

"Such men are paid to risk their lives. Today they earn their keep."

"It's bound to mean more heat."

"I've lived in tropical climates all my life."

"In that case we'll be on our way."

"See Paco as you leave. He has the information you require."

As the door clicked shut behind them, Feldman glanced at Auerbach silently. The walls had ears, and it would be a grave mistake to criticize Costanza on the threshold of his inner sanctum—much less to debate the feasibility of skipping out and leaving him to plan the raid alone.

Their escort—Paco—met them halfway down the corridor, a slim manila envelope in hand. It fitted in Auerbach's pocket perfectly, without a lump or wrinkle as he smoothed the flap.

Without discussing it, Auerbach knew the various objections Feldman had in mind, and some of them were worth considering. They'd talk about it, as they always did, but Auerbach had made his mind up to proceed.

For money, and the power it could buy.

Costanza would be grateful when they pulled it off, and gratitude possessed a price tag in the dealer's world. When they had nailed the loose ends down, Trans-Global would be in a safe position to decide exactly what that price should be.

Retreating toward the gray Mercedes, feeling several pairs of eyes on him, Auerbach circled to the left-hand side and cut his partner off. "I'll drive," he said.

DESPITE THE RECENT truce, Raul Rodriguez knew enough to watch his back. Costanza had been known to change his mind about peace treaties in the past, and strange things had been happening in Medellín—around the world, in fact—the past several days. It seemed that no one was secure, not even if a man was president.

The meeting with Costanza had been reassuring, in a way. Luis had been convincing in his plea of innocence to the attacks on Rodriguez and Mercado. Still, if he wasn't responsible, who was?

At first Rodriguez had believed the justice minister— Benito Franco—might have sponsored the attacks, a desperate politician trying extralegal means to score unprecedented gains against the cartel. That fantasy had died with Franco, and the raids were still continuing.

Rodriguez felt the need of a vacation, somewhere safe and far away, but he couldn't afford to leave his network in the hands of someone less responsible. Whatever happened next, he meant to stay on top of it and counterpunch with everything he had until the opposition was eliminated.

The first step would be picking out his enemies. Retaliation was a waste of time unless he knew the people he was trying to destroy. At this point no one was above suspicion.

Absolutely no one.

Even if Costanza seemed to be a friend in need.

Rodriguez pushed a button on his intercom, and Lupe Vargas answered from the anteroom.

"Sir?"

"The car. I'm going home."

"At once."

The dealer rose and slipped on his lightweight jacket in order to hide the automatic pistol he wore beneath his arm. A pair of bodyguards were waiting for him as he locked the office door. There was no sign of Vargas, and he thought the man must have gone to fetch the car himself.

A loyal subordinate was worth his weight in gold.

They rode the elevator down, emerging into dappled sunlight in the lobby. The limousine was waiting for him at the curb, with Vargas climbing out to get the door.

The rest of it was hazy, bits and pieces like the plate-glass windows that blew inward when the car went up, a ball of fire enveloping the limo, Lupe, everything. The shock wave knocked Rodriguez down, and one of the bodyguards fell across his legs. He could feel the prick of glass shards jutting from his face.

Across the street a woman screamed and kept on screaming as the limo burned. Rodriguez sat up, then struggled to his feet with help from his disheveled troops. A twisted mannequin was burning on the sidewalk, giving off a smell of roasted flesh, and in a flash he knew it was Lupe Vargas gone to hell.

And Rodriguez vowed that someone else would burn in hell before the day was out.

8

The morning light seemed pale and bleak to Dominga Franco. Rising from her lonely bed—where sleep deserted her and she'd never love again—she drew back the curtains but left the windows shut. It was enough to see the people of the city, going on about their lives. She couldn't bear to hear the traffic sounds and laughing voices, too.

For Dominga Franco life had been arrested on the night assassins cut her husband down. If she survived to be a hundred, it would be a mere endurance test, the mechanism of her body functioning without desire, without the best part of her soul.

She would survive, of course; Andeana needed twice the motherly attention now that she'd never see her father's smiling face again. It was a mother's duty to continue for the children, even when her own life lay in tatters on the ground.

The child came first, and that was why she'd decided to leave Medellín. The brutal memories would never go away, but time and distance had a way of mitigating pain. Perhaps someday she'd remember how to sleep and draw a breath without remembering her loss.

Sigfrido had agreed that they should leave. His grief was nearly equal to her own, but Dominga was relying on the gray-haired trooper for her strength and solace in this time of trial.

Her parents were expecting them in Bogotá that afternoon, and they'd leave immediately for a cruise of the

Caribbean. Her father was successful in his own right, a retired executive, but he'd earned his money honestly—without cocaine—and he'd revered Benito almost as a son by birth instead of marriage.

When Sigfrido knocked, she'd already finished dressing, brushing on sufficient makeup to disguise the pallor of her cheeks, the smudges underneath her eyes. A brave face for the world and for her child.

"Time for breakfast, Dominga."

"Please, come in."

Sigfrido's face was drawn and haggard, sculpted in a dour expression of concern.

"You slept?"

"An hour or two," she lied, not wanting him to worry any more than necessary. "And Andeana?"

"In her room. She has an appetite at least."

"The young are strong."

"She might not fully understand."

"Do you?"

Sigfrido's face went hard, his dark eyes chiseled out of flint. "I know the man I blame. He'll burn in hell one day."

"Not soon enough."

"Perhaps. Come have your breakfast."

Dominga shook her head. "I feel like I've already swallowed stones."

"You need your strength."

"I need my husband."

"Dominga—"

"Very well." She crossed the room and joined him at the door. "How long until we leave?"

"Two hours, three. The pilot's a friend of mine. He'll wait."

"I wish you were coming with us."

"There's work to do in Medellín," he told her. "I have debts to pay."

"You loved him, too."

"Benito was a man with many friends."

"But you were special to us both."

The trooper's eyes were brimming as he answered. "You'll be avenged. I promise on the Virgin's sacred heart."

"Take care, Sigfrido. I can't afford to lose you now."

He seemed about to tell her something, but he changed his mind and used a fingertip to brush the tears away.

"Your breakfast."

"Okay."

They passed her daughter's room, and Dominga hesitated, wondering if she should poke her head inside and spend a moment with Andeana. Sigfrido waited for her, letting her decide, and Dominga finally turned in the direction of the stairs.

Not yet.

There would be time enough to talk when they were airborne. Better yet, when they were safely on the cruise ship, miles and miles away from Medellín and men who had conspired to wreck her life—the same men who might wish her daughter dead as an example to their enemies in government.

Sigfrido had been frank in his assessment of their danger, readily agreeing with her plan to leave the city for a time. If she decided never to return, he'd negotiate the sale of property to her advantage, asking nothing for his time or for himself.

Because he was her friend.

Because, in some strange way, he seemed to share the burden of Benito's death.

The guilt wasn't expressed in words, but Dominga saw it in his eyes each time Sigfrido looked at her. He felt responsible, as if he had the power to avert disaster by himself. There was nothing she could say or do to ease his pain. Not while her own was still so fresh.

Perhaps, she thought, in time. But first she had her private grief to cope with, and her child's.

THE SHORT PROCESSION rolled at three o'clock, presumably delayed by packing and arrangements for the flight. The lead car was an unmarked DAS sedan with two men in the front and three more in the back, all armed. The woman and her daughter were sandwiched in the middle vehicle—a limousine—with three more guns. A final complement of four armed men brought up the rear, a four-door compact chosen for its speed and handling.

Auerbach had the three cars covered as they started for the airport, forty minutes out of town, but he left nothing to the vagaries of chance. The ambush site had been selected with precision, and the grim Israeli kept in touch with Feldman via radio as he pursued the convoy north. The trap was ready, waiting for the prey to blunder in.

North of Medellín, the highway leading to the airport passed through two large shantytowns where peasants lived in abject poverty, their rancid hovels interspersed with open sewage lines. Dubbed Comuna Nororiental and Comuna Noroccidental, the slums were an enduring legacy of La Violencia, packed with refugees and descendants of refugees from Colombia's ten-year civil war. Inhabitants were subject to disease and chronic malnutrition, their "communities" beset by violent crime and rampant drug abuse. Police patrolled the shantytowns reluctantly, most often in response to some emergency they couldn't ignore. It came as no surprise to anyone that most of those with any income whatsoever worked as prostitutes or flunkies for the cartel.

It was the perfect place to stage an execution or abduction, if you knew your job. And Isaac Auerbach knew his.

He knew, for instance, that the only working telephones for several hundred yards around the ambush site were pay phones situated in a handful of surrounding shops. An hour prior to contact two of his employees made the rounds, disabling each in turn by clipping wires and squirting instant glue inside the coin slots. Repairmen took their own sweet time to deal with problems in the slums, once they were notified, and that might take a week or more.

Meanwhile, if any of the unavoidable eyewitnesses were fool enough to get involved and summon the police, they'd be forced to make the call from somewhere else...which gave the hit team precious time to carry out their task.

It wouldn't be an easy tag. The tough Israeli made a point of always being honest with himself. His soldiers would be facing down a dozen guns in able hands, and all three cars were radio-equipped. It would be difficult, if not impossible, to stop a call for reinforcements from getting through, but any backup teams would have to arm themselves and make the trip from Medellín by land or air, if they had helicopters standing by.

In either case, too late.

It would have been a simpler task to kill the woman and her child instead of taking them alive, but they were useless to Costanza in the ground. He wanted something he could bargain with, some leverage against the government in Bogotá, and it was Auerbach's job to carry out instructions from the top.

It didn't matter that he thought Costanza was mistaken on the Bogotá connection. Never mind that his employer was about to escalate hostilities with the elected government. It was Costanza's call, and Auerbach could always tuck the hostages away somewhere until he had been paid. It was a risky game, but one Costanza understood.

And afterward, with money in his pocket, there would be sufficient time for reassessment of their situation, weighing odds and angles to decide if they should stay or leave Colombia for some new climate where the heat was less intense.

Sufficient time to save himself, at least, before the ship went down.

Extraction of the targets would be Feldman's job, with Auerbach acting in a supervisory capacity. He knew the younger mercenary viewed the mission as a foolish risk, but Feldman would conduct himself as a professional.

Auerbach was half a mile behind his prey when Feldman sprang the trap. A garbage truck cut off the point car, veering right across the road before its driver killed the engine, simulating breakdown. Forced to stop, the convoy was prevented from retreating when a pair of rented vehicles appeared and blocked the lanes behind.

By that time gunners armed with automatic weapons were erupting from the garbage truck, more soldiers pouring from the cars in back, pedestrians on either side producing guns concealed in bags or parcels hidden underneath their shirts and jackets. There were twenty-seven men, including Feldman, with another dozen waiting in reserve if things went wrong.

The DAS commandos knew their business, laying down a screen of fire that killed three members of the strike force in as many seconds, but they were outnumbered and outgunned. The point and tail cars started taking hits immediately, snipers laying off the limousine on pain of execution if they harmed the woman or her child. As Auerbach's driver parked a block uprange behind the two-car barricade, they had a fair view of the action through binoculars.

He saw the shotgun rider from the point car leave his vehicle, a crouching figure with a submachine gun in his hands. The runner fired a burst in the direction of the garbage truck, a line of bullet marks appearing on the faded paint, and then converging streams of fire ripped through him, spinning him around before he fell.

The point car's driver was already dead, a burst across the windshield shattering his skull in the initial moments of the clash. His lifeless body had slumped forward, and the horn was blaring mindlessly, a one-note musical accompaniment to carnage.

The three guns remaining in the lead car bailed out on either side as snipers made their hiding place untenable. The first man out was clearly dead or dying, shoved ahead of one who held a stubby riot shotgun. The falling body crumpled like a sack of laundry to the pavement, nearly tripping up the next man out, but he recovered swiftly, hopping twice on one foot to regain his balance, squeezing off a blast that dropped his nearest adversary and an innocent civilian side by side. He sprinted for the cover of a nearby storefront, but the enemy had found the range by then, and he was cut down in his tracks.

The sole survivor from the point car dropped and wriggled underneath his vehicle for cover, cringing as a burst of ricochets struck sparks across the pavement, hammering the undercarriage. Another burst ripped through the fuel tank, spilling gasoline beneath the car, where more sparks ignited it a moment later.

Auerbach was watching as the human torch erupted from his hiding place, flames streaming out behind him as he ran. Another moment and the car exploded. The concussion bowled him over, but he came up screaming, beating at the fire that consumed his flesh. The snipers could have dropped him, but he posed no further threat, and so they let him run.

The tail car's driver, meanwhile, had attempted to reverse direction, but a bullet ripped his lower jaw away and pitched him across the shotgun rider's lap. The engine stalled and died as automatic fire began to drill the compact vehicle from every side.

The right-hand door sprang open, and the shotgun rider scrambled clear, bright streaks of crimson soaking through his slacks and jacket. The driver's blood was mingled with his own as a half-dozen snipers riddled him from different angles, dropping him beside the car.

The backseat gunners bailed out on the right, one close behind the other, seeking cover in between their own car and the limousine. They both had automatic rifles, spraying shops along the street in search of targets, wounding several passersby. The peasants were expendable, and they were fighting for their lives.

Three gunners rushed them, one retreating with a flesh wound after his companions were cut down. It took a 40 mm high-explosive charge to root them out, Feldman's grenade launcher scoring a direct hit on the compact and reducing it to twisted scrap.

Two minutes and eleven seconds into the attack the limo occupants were on their own.

SIGFRIDO WAS PREPARED for trouble in the same way that he always took precautions when he dealt with members of the cartel. The murder of Benito Franco should have theoretically removed his family from the line of fire, but narco-barons like Costanza sometimes nursed a grudge beyond all reason, spanning generations in their hunger for revenge.

Sigfrido knew that Dominga Franco and her daughter wouldn't be entirely safe while they remained inside the borders of Colombia. Together they comprised a symbol of the nation's shame, and there were men at large who wished them dead because of that. For others it would be enough that Dominga's husband had opposed the ruling drug cartel, despite the fact that he'd paid for that decision with his life.

As for their safety once they left the country... Who could say? Costanza's gunmen were routinely active in America, and one ex-minister of justice had been murdered on a street in Budapest a short time after his appointment as ambassador to Hungary.

Outside Colombia the task of guarding Dominga and Andeana Franco would belong to someone else. A feeling of relief was instantly replaced by guilt, Sigfrido understanding that his friendship for the murdered minister of justice called for more than a perfunctory disposal of his wife and child.

The only sure protection for them now would lie in the elimination of Costanza and his syndicate. It seemed a fantasy, and yet there *was* a man who might be equal to the task. The tall American in whom Benito had placed his trust the last few days before he was cut down. The stranger hadn't saved Benito's life, but he'd wreaked a bloody vengeance on the killers, and Sigfrido knew he wasn't finished yet. It might be possible to strike a bargain with the dark man, pass along strategic information from the DAS or lend support against the common enemy. Discovery of their collusion would result in Sigfrido's swift dismissal—possibly in prosecution—but the risk would be worthwhile if it obtained results.

His mind was on the future when the garbage truck loomed out of nowhere, stalling in the middle of the street and forcing their procession to a halt. A glance behind them showed him two cars blocking their angle of retreat, and then the shooting started, automatic weapons hammering the point and tail cars, scattering pedestrians on both sides of the street.

The limousine was armor-plated, fitted with gun ports, fire extinguishers, and tires designed to absorb multiple hits without deflating. Even so, Sigfrido pushed his frightened charges to the floor and kept them there, unlimbering the CAR-15 concealed beneath his seat. In front the driver was intent on looking for an exit, while the shotgun rider palmed the dashboard microphone and beamed a Mayday signal back to Medellín.

How long until reinforcements came?

Perhaps too long.

The first grenade impacted on their right front fender, detonating with a blast that shook the car and nearly deafened everyone inside. The shotgun rider started shouting at the microphone, held inches from his lips, as if the ringing in his ears somehow affected those on the receiving end. Sigfrido thrust the muzzle of his carbine through the nearest gun port, squeezing off a burst that shattered window glass across the street, spent casings pooled around his feet.

The next explosion took their right rear wheel and wrenched it off the axle, the DAS man sliding as the vehicle began to list. The driver kept on trying to escape, convinced he could drive on three wheels if he had to, but a third grenade removed the option, flashing on the pavement underneath the limo's grille. The big car lurched and shuddered like a wounded rhino, and the engine died.

Sigfrido thought of firing a complaint off to the manufacturer, but he'd have to be alive for that, and at the moment he wouldn't have bet a peso on their chances for escape. The limo seemed immune to sniper fire, but it was going nowhere fast, and he could smell the stench of burning gasoline. It might have been the point and tail cars burning, but Sigfrido couldn't take the chance.

He leaned across the front seat, past the shaken driver, jabbing with the muzzle of his weapon toward a button on the dash. On contact fire-retardant chemicals were instantly released beneath the hood, around the gas tank and along the undercarriage of the damaged limousine. It seemed to work, but they could only use the system once without recharging the extinguishers.

A new explosion rocked the car, this one behind him, and the trunk lid crumpled like a sheet of tin beneath the impact of a heavy fist. How many more could they withstand?

A muffled voice was calling for their surrender, and Sigfrido recognized the flat sound of a megaphone. If they didn't come out at once it warned, the car would be destroyed with everyone inside.

And if they did . . . what, then?

Across the street a man in denim overalls was moving closer to the limousine. Sigfrido noted something on his back, secured with shoulder straps, a sticklike object in his hands.

At twenty feet he recognized the flamethrower for what it was.

They could surrender, or be baked alive. Unless . . .

"Stay here," Sigfrido warned the others as he cracked his door, the CAR-15 forgotten on the seat behind him. Stepping clear, he wrinkled his nose at the pervasive smell of motor oil and roasting flesh.

He had one chance, and only one.

The Browning automatic was an easy draw, his holster custom-made for speed. From twenty feet away he made allowance for the longer pull of double-action firing, making every fraction of a second count. The denim-clad man with the flamethrower had been expecting mute surrender, and he stopped three parabellum rounds above the waist before he knew he was dead.

Sigfrido heard the crack of gunfire, felt a heavy blow against one shoulder blade. The pavement rose to meet him, and his automatic clattered in the street beyond his reach.

No pain, at first, but it would come.

Before he closed his eyes the trooper looked for comfort in the fact that he'd done his best.

But it hadn't been good enough.

DOMINGA FRANCO HEARD the final burst of shots and huddled on the floor beside Andeana, afraid to look outside. Another moment and the guns would be directed at the limousine, a storm of bullets would find its way inside and snuff out their lives.

But nothing happened.

Rather, there was no more shooting as the gunmen saw their chance to rush the crippled car. One of them reached inside Sigfrido's door and dragged his rifle out, a submachine gun covering the guards up front. A gruff voice ordered them outside, and fingers gripped her arm when she was sluggish in response.

On foot beside the car she glimpsed Sigfrido's body on the pavement, trying to protect Andeana from the sight. There were too many corpses in the street for her to screen them all.

A pair of gunmen flanked the woman and her child, propelling them across the street and past a bullet-riddled shop, around the corner to a waiting car. Before they reached it

Dominga heard another burst of automatic fire from the direction of the limousine. She didn't have to turn around to know the driver and her last surviving bodyguard were dead.

With equal certainty she knew these men—or others like them—were responsible for snuffing out her husband's life. At first it puzzled her to realize they were still alive... and then confusion turned to fear.

She could expect no mercy from her enemies. They would destroy her, kill her only child without a second thought. Their hesitation indicated other motives, and the thought of being taken hostage made her blood run cold.

But they were still alive, and life meant hope—for now.

If she was very lucky, Dominga thought she might be privileged to meet her husband's murderer, the man who sat at home and ordered good men killed. One chance to reach the bastard's eyes, and she wouldn't begrudge her death, a chance to mark the animal who had destroyed her life, and make him understand real pain.

Inside the car she slipped an arm around Andeana's tiny shoulders, pulled her close and whispered in her ear, "We'll be all right," she said. "A little ride, that's all. There's a man we have to meet."

9

Sigfrido focused on the acoustic tiles above his head and realized he was still alive. He tried to move but found his arms and legs immobilized. In momentary panic he believed he was paralyzed, but careful flexing of his limbs revealed that both his arms had been secured with straps; his legs were pinned beneath the sheets and blankets of a well-made bed.

A hospital.

In Medellín?

Sigfrido sought to turn his head and found the effort almost more than he could manage. There was pain, in spite of the sedative that made his brain feel wrapped in cotton wool. His mouth was dry, and when he called for help, his voice emerged somewhere between a whisper and a croak.

The nurse was instantly beside him, offering a plastic cup of water with a flexi-straw that let him drink while lying on his back. It nearly choked him, even so, and she withdrew the cup before he had a chance to drink his fill.

"No more," she cautioned, reaching down to take his pulse.

Sigfrido knew he was badly injured. How many times had he been hit? The worst pain radiated from his back and abdomen, but something also burned inside one thigh, above the knee.

If he survived, it would be something he could tell the others back at work. Luis Costanza did his best, and still the bastard couldn't—

Wait!

He whispered Dominga's name, and the nurse retreated, a strange expression on her face.

A shadow fell across the bed. Sigfrido recognized the doctor by his gown and stethoscope, a man no more than half his age. A child in terms of life experience.

"Are you in pain?"

Sigfrido shook his head and whispered Dominga's name again. The doctor let him have another sip of water; more this time, but not enough to ease the burning in his throat.

"You have insistent visitors," the doctor said. "Police, I think. The choice is yours, but I'd like to send them home and have them call another time."

From the expression on the doctor's face, Sigfrido thought there might not be another time. "I'll see them now."

"Not long. You need your strength."

The doctor moved beyond his line of sight and was replaced a moment later by two men in business suits—an Hispanic stranger and the tall American.

"I'm dying," he informed them.

"Yes," the American said. "They've got a priest outside."

"Too late." Sigfrido's smile had more in common with a grimace. "Dominga?"

"Gone. The child, as well."

"Not dead?"

"We'll have to wait and see."

"It was Costanza."

"Yes."

"He knew where we were going. Traitors everywhere."

"I'd like to try to get them back. If you can tell us anything at all . . ."

Sigfrido thought about it for a moment, waiting for the germ of an idea to surface in his mind. "A foreigner was in charge. The voice was wrong for a Colombian."

"Wrong how?"

"He knew the Spanish, but his accent...maybe European, or the Middle East."

"You're sure?"

A decent question. With the megaphone a voice would be distorted over distance.

Sigfrido nodded. *"Sí."*

"His face?"

"I never saw it. You must...punish..."

Suddenly the pain came back in force, stretching his lips in the outline of a scream. Sigfrido found another hand and clutched it tightly, waiting for the scream to break, humiliated when it came out as a rasping sigh.

He heard the tall man's voice as if from miles away, but he couldn't make out the words. The American's eyes reached out to touch his own, and then the lights began to fail.

"YOUR BUDDY AUERBACH?" Grimaldi asked.

Across the room Katz shrugged. "Or Feldman. Either way it's all the same."

"They made the snatch, then?"

Bolan cleared his throat. "We go on that assumption until we're proved wrong. You know damn well Costanza didn't make the tag himself."

"Why grab the womenfolk?" James asked.

"Why not?" McCarter answered with a question of his own. "The cartel prides itself on blitzing families. Scorched earth."

"We would have found their bodies at the scene if Costanza only wanted revenge."

"What, then?" McCarter asked.

"A lever maybe," Bolan replied. "If Costanza's getting desperate—and we'd better hope he is—he might be grabbing straws. A local hero's wife and child could buy him room to breathe, a little extra time. He can't be sure who's hitting him, or why. With leverage he could make the DAS find out."

"Which means we end up sparring with the government," Grimaldi said.

"Worst case, it's possible. Unless we stop him first."

The gruff Israeli cleared his throat. "I hate to move against Costanza with the woman and her child in jeopardy."

"We might not have a choice . . . but I was thinking of a way to get them back."

"From Auerbach?"

"It's worth a shot."

"He's gone to ground," Grimaldi countered. "The guy's like smoke if you try to pin him down."

"Somebody knows exactly where he is," the Executioner reminded them.

"Costanza, sure," James said.

"And Feldman," Katz added.

"What kind of progress are we making with the second-in-command?" Bolan asked.

The Israeli frowned. "McPherson's got his men staked out around the downtown offices. If Auerbach or Feldman show, we'll get a call. I wouldn't hold my breath."

"We need to stir things up," Bolan said. "One way to smoke out the players is by giving them a different problem they can focus on. I'd say we've gone too long without a taste of civil war."

"Rodriguez and Mercado?" James questioned.

"They'll be simmering by now," Bolan said. "Enough to doubt Costanza, anyway. I doubt we'll have to push them very far."

"What kind of pushing did you have in mind?"

"This time I want it synchronized. No question that they've got an army breathing down their necks. If we play it right, Costanza comes off smelling, but it won't be like a rose."

Katz lit a cigarette and stared at Bolan through the rising smoke. "And if we turn up Auerbach or Feldman in the meantime?"

"We take them down, breathing if possible. I want to find out if the hostages are still alive, and where they're being held."

"We're working from the padre's list, I take it," Grimaldi said.

"For a start. We'll pick up other targets as we go along."

"We might not get them back, you know," McCarter pointed out.

"In that case someone owes us double. Right?"

"Suits me."

"At least we've finished part of it," Encizo said. "Caseros, and the business in Miami."

Bolan scanned the ring of solemn faces. "Nothing's finished with Costanza still alive. He'll patch up the whole damn network within a month unless we take him out."

"Let's do it, then," McCarter said.

"But carefully," Bolan warned.

"What's shaking with F-2 and DAS?" Gary Manning asked.

"Everybody's busy pointing fingers at the other guy," Grimaldi said. "You talk about a cluster-fuck. These bozos know positions no one's ever tried in Washington."

"That bad?" Katz asked.

"And then some. Figure—what?—a third of each department on somebody's pad, for starters. Those who try to play it straight are swimming upstream all the time. I've got a feeling the academy provides a course on how to make excuses when you fail."

"We've seen it all before," Bolan said. "Nothing changes but the names."

The plain fact was, they did have victories from time to time, but there was no such thing as a final victory in an everlasting war.

"If we're doing it," James said, "I guess we ought to get it done."

And so they did.

No MATTER what his partner said, the heat was different this time. Feldman recognized the fact that they were in too deep, but he seemed powerless to turn the game around, much less since they had personally grabbed the widow and her child.

With other clients they'd followed many of the same procedures, training thugs and peasants to be mercenaries, bodyguards, assassins—but Costanza wanted more. Each time he handed over cash, the dealer let you know in subtle ways—a crooked smile, his tone of voice—that he was buying more than just the services of a professional.

A soul perhaps.

Chaim Feldman wasn't a religious man. Since leaving Israel, he'd set foot in a synagogue no more than a half-dozen times, and then for funerals. He gave no thought at all to problems of the afterlife, reward or punishment by an unforgiving God. He'd inflicted death too often for it to remain a mystery.

But since Auerbach had signed Trans-Global with the Medellín cartel, he'd been feeling trapped. The level of involvement had begun to escalate at once, from training gunmen to directing their activities and supervising raids. By chance they'd been spared direct participation in the murder of Benito Franco, but the massacre of state police and the abduction of his family would be enough to place them both in front of a firing squad if they were caught.

Assuming they were taken in alive.

The heat was everywhere, but life went on...for some. Instead of going underground and seeking shelter in the company of soldiers he'd trained, he was assigned to visit the Trans-Global offices and sanitize their files in preparation for the worst. Auerbach wouldn't admit it—even to himself perhaps—but *he* was having second thoughts about Colombia, as well.

Too late?

They still might have a chance to save themselves, but they were wasting precious time.

It was a given that Costanza would pursue them if they fled, when he had time and troops available. Of course, as things stood now, there was a decent chance he wouldn't survive the coming storm. Gonzalo Rodriguez Gacha had been killed for less, and the security police were primed for battle at the moment, with a dozen of their fellows lying dead in Medellín.

All things considered, though, it might be easier for Auerbach and Feldman to eliminate Costanza themselves. A simple business meeting, in and out before the watchdogs found out what was happening.

The parking lot was nearly full, but Feldman found a place and locked the gray Mercedes, activating the alarm. No high-explosive party favors would be waiting for him when he slid behind the wheel again and turned the key.

Upstairs he found their secretary thumbing through a magazine and looking bored. Trans-Global got perhaps a dozen calls each week, from salesmen and prospective clients, all of whom were courteously turned away. A walk-in off the street would be unprecedented, and the girl looked startled for a moment, visibly relaxing as she recognized her boss.

"No calls today?"

She shook her head. "No, sir."

"That's fine."

He used his key and stepped inside the private office, moving toward a pair of filing cabinets on the wall beside his desk. The files were duplicates and dummies, the correct originals sequestered in a safe-deposit box downtown, but it was possible that some of them could indicate at least a theoretical connection with Costanza and his syndicate.

They had to go.

It took the best part of an hour with the modern shredder, but he got it done. Manila folders and their contents were processed into drab confetti while he watched. It was a tiresome job, but one he dared not delegate to a subordinate.

Emerging from the office, Feldman paused to lock the door behind him, then pocketed the key. The secretary offered him a smile, which he returned.

"You might as well go home, Maria ... with a full day's pay, of course."

"Thank you, Mr. Feldman."

"It's okay."

Waiting for the elevator, Feldman wondered how much longer Auerbach would wait before he made his mind up whether they should go or stay. If he delayed much longer, Feldman was prepared to make the jump himself. Let Isaac hold a grudge if he was so inclined.

The trees aside, Colombia reminded him increasingly of Lebanon, where anarchy had come to be accepted as a daily fact of life. If there were any winners in the game, they must be those who managed to survive with something of their dignity intact.

A born survivor, Feldman meant to walk away from Medellín before he had to be carried away. Colombia wasn't his homeland, and he felt no sentimental need to help the peasants—or the narcobarons—fight their local wars. Beyond a certain point the risks outweighed the rewards, and it was time to cut his losses while he had a chance.

Two men were waiting for him when the elevator door slid open, hard-eyed gringos like himself. Instinctively he punched the button for another floor, but one of them had blocked the door, his right hand tucked inside the jacket that concealed a shoulder holster. The second man had also slipped the buttons on his blazer, standing ready for a draw in case his partner missed.

"We're going for a little ride," the first man said. His accent might have been American, but Feldman couldn't pin it down with any certainty.

"There must be some mistake."

"You made it, working for Costanza."

"Who?"

"You've got a choice here—either make it on your own or we can carry you. But first I'll have to do your knees."

"I'm capable of walking by myself."

"Let's see a sample, then."

They had the lobby to themselves, and Feldman followed orders, standing with his palms against the wall, legs spread, while he was patted down. They found the Walther automatic on his belt and made it disappear, together with the stiletto in its ankle sheath.

Outside, they marched him to a nondescript sedan and placed him in the back seat, snapping handcuffs on his wrists, the chain looped through an armrest on the nearest door. If Feldman tried, he could release the latch, but opening the door would merely plunge him into the street while they were driving, crushing him beneath the wheels or dragging him along the pavement until they chose to stop.

It was a loser's gambit either way.

His captors weren't Colombian, so they wouldn't be police. Americans had no authority to make arrests on foreign soil, and Feldman would retain the finest lawyers in the capital to fight them all the way.

Unless . . .

It struck him that they might not be police from *any* jurisdiction, and his blood ran cold.

"Where are you taking me? Who are you?"

He caught the driver grinning at him in the rearview mirror.

"Just relax, old son. Enjoy the ride."

IN PREPARATION for the grilling, they'd rigged a walk-in closet in the safehouse to accommodate the needs of an interrogation chamber. It would never qualify as soundproof, but the walls were stout enough and reinforced with thrift shop mattresses. No windows looked out on the outside world. They'd have privacy enough, and if the neighbors heard a yelp or two, they were unlikely to involve themselves.

Yakov Katzenelenbogen frowned on torture—both for its brutality and unreliability—but he was also conscious of the need for answers in a hurry. Feldman would be given every opportunity to talk without resort to pain, but he *would* talk, regardless of the means required to loosen his tongue.

They needed Auerbach's location, with the woman and her child, before they could proceed against Costanza. Any risk of harm to Dominga Franco or her daughter would be weighed against the larger goal of breaking the cartel. With luck they might be able to retrieve the hostages alive.

If it wasn't too late.

Chaim Feldman was a younger version of the one-eyed Auerbach—Israeli paratroop, a tour of duty with the Mossad before he chose a mercenary life-style and began to shop around for clients in a world at war. He hadn't duplicated Auerbach's conflict with authorities in Israel; rather, it appeared that Feldman made his choice on more pragmatic grounds, with ready cash in mind.

But he was still a killer, hardened in the border wars and antiterrorist campaigns that never seemed to end in Israel. Since departing from his homeland, joining Auerbach in Trans-Global, he had worked throughout the Middle East and Africa before expanding to the Western Hemisphere. Wherever he appeared, men learned to kill their fellows more efficiently.

And others died.

Abducting female hostages would be brand-new lows for Auerbach and company, but Katz never doubted their involvement in the raid. When they began to take their orders from Luis Costanza, they'd crossed the line from simple mercenaries, living on the edge, to henchmen of a far-flung criminal cartel. They'd been paid to risk their lives, and Katz would have no qualms about eliminating either man if called upon to do so.

Starting now.

The Mounties had delivered Feldman and removed themselves. Katz found him in the closet, stripped down to his shorts, secured to a chair with lengths of nylon clothesline wrapped around his ankles, wrists and chest. No sign of recognition showed on his face as Katz joined him.

"I demand to know what's happening," the captive said.

"It should be obvious," Katz said. "We need some information you possess, and we're prepared to spend the necessary time retrieving it."

Suspicion clouded Feldman's eyes. "What information?"

"Auerbach's location for a start. The woman and her daughter if they're still alive."

"I don't know what you mean."

"Know this. I'm not a patient man, especially where baby killers are concerned. I'm frankly hoping you'll resist a bit to make it sporting."

"You're making a mistake."

"We'll see."

Katz snapped his fingers, stepping to the side as Gary Manning wheeled a handcart past him, stopping just in front of Feldman's chair. An auto battery was fastened to the cart with frayed elastic heavy-duty jumper cables looped around the grips on top.

"I don't know anyone named Auerbach," the captive told him, staring at the battery. "As for a woman—"

"It's peculiar, don't you think? A man of your intelligence not knowing who his business partners are?"

"I run Trans-Global by myself."

"Of course."

Katz picked up the jumper cables and stretched them out across the floor at Feldman's feet. He took his time attaching heavy alligator clips to the battery terminals, using insulated grips to lift the free ends, holding them an inch or two apart.

"I doubt if this will kill you outright. I'll be disappointed if it does. The battery may suffer, but we have a spare."

As Katz spoke, he brushed the metal clips together, dousing Feldman with a shower of sparks that made him flinch. The ropes held fast, and while he wriggled fiercely in the chair, he had no prospect for escape.

"Once more—your partner's address?"

"Go to hell."

"You first."

Katz pinched the handles of the black clip, fastening the ragged jaws to Feldman's left big toe. The bite was painful in itself, a foretaste of the agony to come. He switched the red clip to his left hand, reaching out with his prosthesis for the snug elastic waist of Feldman's shorts.

"For God's sake, don't!"

"We're all agnostics here," Katz answered.

The elastic snapped, and so did Feldman's nerve.

"All right! I'll tell you what you want to know!"

"Okay, I'm waiting," the gruff Israeli muttered.

10

The breeding ground for crime in Medellín lay west of downtown in the teeming neighborhood dubbed Barrio Antioquia. Officially declared a red-light district in the 1950s, the slum harbored countless prostitutes of both sexes, dwelling side by side with other men and women who had lost their human values in the crunch between cocaine and urban poverty. Almost without exception perpetrators of most outrageous crimes in Medellín—and foreign gunners in the stateside cocaine wars—were drawn from the population of Barrio Antioquia. Hired killers from the district operated on sliding price scales, ranging from a hundred dollars on domestic homicides into the low five figures for celebrities and government officials. Gunmen from the district didn't take offense if they were asked to execute a random "practice killing" as a show of faith.

It was the perfect neighborhood in which to stash a powder factory, and Father Julio Lazaro had provided Bolan with the address of a lab maintained by Raul Rodriguez near the old, abandoned airport that had once served downtown Medellín.

The guards would be a problem, but he compensated by adopting a disguise. His army surplus jacket had been torn and patched in several places, and his denim jeans had lost their shape from too much wear. The garments were deliberately unkempt and reeked of sweat. The rest of Bolan's camouflage consisted of strategic grit and grime, a tattered baseball cap and an affected slouch that shaved two inches off his height.

If anyone was startled by the sight of Bolan stepping from a shiny rental car and moving off along the street, they kept their questions to themselves. For all the locals knew, he could have been a hustler, possibly a runner for the syndicate. The quickest way to lose your life in Barrio Antioquia was to butt into someone else's business, when that business might be drugs or homicide.

With Jack Grimaldi at the wheel the rental car moved on and disappeared beyond the second intersection down. If all went well, the pilot would complete a four-block circuit, giving Bolan time for his approach, and plant himself outside the target building once the Executioner had made his way inside.

From that point on they'd be playing it by ear.

If there were sentries posted on the street, they hid themselves well. No one appeared to notice Bolan as he passed the target building, veering to his left and moving down a cluttered alley just beyond. The fire escape was rusty, but it held his weight and the warrior reached the third-floor landing unopposed.

The windows had been painted over to discourage prying eyes, but two of them were standing open in concession to the muggy afternoon, providing extra ventilation for the lab. It would have paid to put a spotter on the fire escape, but passing time and lack of major opposition in the barrio had seemingly convinced Rodriguez that he could operate with virtual impunity.

It would be Bolan's pleasure to inform him otherwise.

The open window offered him a glimpse inside. Half a dozen men in lab coats worked around long tables, mixing chemicals and sifting powder, weighing plastic bags and jotting down the figures in a loose-leaf notebook. Near the exit Bolan marked a pair of gunners, and he knew there had to be more outside.

He fished inside the baggy pockets of his coat, removing plastic goggles and a surgeon's mask. The mini-Uzi and its custom silencer were next, immediately followed by a frag grenade.

The warrior didn't know the men inside the lab, but he knew their type. Obsessed with wealth and status, they'd murder thousands to achieve a certain life-style in Colombia or the United States. Some did their killing with a gun, while others used a beaker and a Bunsen burner. But it all came out the same. Their victims suffered physical addiction, gross humiliation and untimely death.

The lab rats had a debt to pay, and Bolan was about to call in their markers.

He pulled the pin on the grenade and lobbed it through the open window, aiming for the table with its bright array of glassware, ducking back and down the fire escape to miss the blast.

Four seconds.

The goggles spared his eyes, but he was showered by a storm of broken glass as four large windows buckled, shattered by a clap of thunder from within. He gave the shrapnel two more beats to find its mark, then rushed the nearest empty window frame and threw himself inside.

His pitch had fallen short, but it made little difference in the confines of the lab. The warrior came out of a shoulder roll to find the nearest table lying on its side, a storm of crystal powder swirling in the air. At least two men were down and thrashing in the middle of it all, with others staggering around the room and clutching bloody wounds or shaking heads to counter the concussion of the blast.

He didn't give them time, the Uzi tracking left to right and spraying death around the room. The gunners were first, one of them brandishing an automatic while his sidekick stood there, looking dazed. The Uzi played no favorites, and the two of them went down together, spouting crimson from a line of bullet tracks.

The lab men took another moment of his time—three up, three down, before the last one on his feet attempted to escape by leaping headfirst through a window. There was no fire escape outside to catch him, and his shriek of panic ended when he hit the pavement below.

The outside gunners took a moment to respond, and Bolan fed the Uzi a fresh clip while he waited. He was ready when the door flew open, three tough men rushing through with guns in hand. They came in braced for damn near anything... except the storm of parabellum manglers that quickly dropped the first two in their tracks.

The last one in was faster, dodging backward, but he made the move too late to save himself. A short precision burst ripped through the wooden door as he was leaving, and the Executioner was suddenly alone.

He passed on the incendiaries, taking time to find a jug of hydrochloric acid on the shelf and pour its contents over much of the cocaine already scattered on the floor. Then he cleared the empty room outside and moved along a hallway, eyeing numbered doors on both sides. The other tenants seemed to be away from home, or else they chose to let the sounds of combat die away before they ventured out to check the damage.

On the stairs he met a sallow-faced gunner coming up, a shiny autoloader in his fist.

"*¿Qué pasa?*"

Bolan let him have a 3-round burst that slammed him backward, tumbling awkwardly until he hit the landing and collapsed there in a heap. No further opposition greeted him as he hustled toward the street and found Grimaldi waiting.

"So how'd it go?" the pilot asked.

"It went. Let's try for two."

The rental nosed out into traffic, moving toward another front in Bolan's war.

"YOU FIRST," Calvin James ordered, nudging Feldman from the car.

It was a physical relief to stretch his legs, but the sensation meant no more to Feldman at the moment than an errant breeze across his face. Instead, he concentrated on the extra weight around his hips, the chafing of a heavy belt secured with a padlock that had grated on his tailbone since he'd crawled inside the car.

"Just keep your jacket buttoned," he'd been advised. "You'll do all right unless you try to run or take it off yourself."

Not likely with twenty pounds of C-4 plastique strapped around his waist and primed to detonate on radio command.

The belt wouldn't be tamper-proof, of course—an expert would have found some way around the crude security devices—but he simply didn't have the luxury of time. They told him that the detonator was effective in a half-mile radius, and Feldman had no reason to dispute that claim or put it to the test.

He moved along the crowded sidewalk, desperately afraid of being jostled, with his escort hanging back a bit. The black man had a detonator in his pocket, Feldman knew, but it wasn't the only one. Somewhere—perhaps inside the building, parked along the street or strolling in the crowd— were others similarly armed. He might lose one or all of them, if he were clever, but they merely had to touch a button, any one of them, and he was vaporized.

A taxi passed him, heading in the opposite direction, with its driver talking on the radio. The sight made Feldman cringe, intensely conscious of the fact that radio remote controls were subject to sporadic interference that could trigger a device.

Auerbach's command post was the top floor of a luxury downtown apartment house that Costanza owned. His name wasn't recorded on the bogus lease, nor did he pay the monthly rent according to its terms. In fact, the four flats—

one for Auerbach, one for Feldman, two for bodyguards—
were part of their arrangement with the cartel. The guards
on live-in duty were the best Trans-Global had produced
from the available manpower.

It had been difficult for Feldman, giving up his partner to
the enemy, but he'd seen no other options at the time. Survival was the first priority in any given situation, barring
altruistic sacrifice, and Feldman was adept at looking out
for number one.

The worst part, after making up his mind to play along,
had been convincing his abductors that Costanza had the
woman and her child, a transfer carried out by Auerbach on
his own, while Feldman cleaned up after the attack. He
honestly couldn't direct his captors to the hostages.

But Auerbach could.

That solitary fact had been responsible for sparing Feldman's life so far—and it had also placed the high-explosive
belt around his waist. A walking bomb, he'd be serving as
the point man for his enemies when they took Isaac down.

Or tried to take him.

It wouldn't be quite so simple.

The doorman passed him through without a second
glance, and Feldman crossed the lobby to the in-house telephone. He punched a coded number out, and Auerbach
answered on the second ring.

"Hello?"

"I'm coming up."

"You're late."

He had rehearsed the cover story in his mind until he
knew the lie by heart. "There was a salesman pestering
Maria at the office. Stubborn bastard slowed me down."

"No problems otherwise?"

"All clear."

"Okay."

He cradled the receiver, glancing toward the street in time
to see the black man pause outside. As Feldman watched,

he had a brief discussion with the doorman, brandishing credentials that appeared to satisfy the man in uniform.

Before his watchdog entered Feldman was already moving toward the elevator, waiting for the doors to open and receive him. It was no good hoping for the metal elevator shaft to block a signal from the detonator; they'd told him that much on the ride downtown. No line-of-sight connection with the chosen target was required.

The car arrived, the door hissed open and he stepped inside. As he punched the button numbered 9, Feldman could see the black man moving slowly toward him, killing time, one hand inside the pocket of his suit coat, wrapped around the detonator, just in case.

It had occurred to Feldman that the whole damn thing might be a ruse. His captors might not care to speak with Auerbach at all. Wired up the way he was, a human warhead, Feldman made the perfect weapon for assassination. Once he came within a dozen yards of Auerbach, a silent signal from the street below would do the job. No risk whatsoever for the triggerman.

The elevator reached its destination with a lurch, and Feldman caught his breath. C-4 was stable, but he wasn't sure about the detonator wiring on the belt. For all he knew a simple touch might be enough to set the charges off.

The door whisked open on a pastel corridor. Directly opposite, a member of the house security detachment occupied a plastic chair, a porno magazine open on his lap. Beside him, on the floor, a radio was playing a salsa number.

Emerging from the elevator, Feldman grimaced at the music, one hand edging toward his waist before he caught himself. He felt the gunman watching him and pointed at the radio. "I'd turn that off if I were you."

THE DAS CREDENTIALS were authentic, to a point. Provided by a contact on the force, they'd been doctored to identify the men of Phoenix Force as officers of state security. Since three of them spoke decent Spanish, they'd pass a cursory inspection. Gary Manning, the Canadian, was relegated to the role of wheelman for their getaway, and Katz made up his own linguistic gap by pairing with Encizo for the hit.

He could have stayed outside, but leaving Auerbach to other hands wouldn't have satisfied his need to meet the renegade once more, a need that had been burning in his gut since they'd been briefed at Stony Man and he'd seen Auerbach's one-eyed face reflected on the screen.

The sheer intensity of his desire to punish Auerbach had startled Katz, prompting him to look inside himself for motives. The anger was a primal thing, and he had difficulty pinning down its source.

He knew it wasn't the mercenary's life-style that turned his stomach. Countless soldiers went in search of private wars when they'd outlived their usefulness at home, addicted to the thrill of combat or the opportunity to test themselves in situations where the stakes were always life and death. A number of them lost direction in the process, turning to the highest bidder in defiance of their personal beliefs—while others had no personal ideals to sacrifice. From time to time they crossed the path of Phoenix Force, and they were swiftly dealt with if they came as enemies. But none before had stirred such indignation in the gruff Israeli's heart.

His personal connection with the enemy was part of it this time, but there was more involved than simple disappointment in a former comrade. Auerbach's career, in many ways, provided Katzenelenbogen with a mirror image of his own. Both men had been part of Israel's struggle to survive, and both had been gravely wounded in the Six-Day War. Emerging from the hospital with wounds that qualified them both for pensions, they'd joined the Mossad instead to carry on the fight. In time both Katz and Auerbach had left their country's service, moving on to search for other enemies and other battlefields.

Considered from a distance, they might easily have passed for twins—but there were differences, as well. While Katz had turned his hand to stalking terrorists and criminals in private practice, Auerbach became their tool and confidant, employed by animals he would have shot on sight without a second thought while he was working for the Mossad. Unlike the mercs who lost their way in search of thrills or one last payoff, Auerbach had given up his very soul.

And there—except for some controlling force he couldn't identify, much less explain—went Katz himself.

He needed to eliminate his former comrade as a gesture to himself, a means of validating choices he'd made in the past few years. Auerbach couldn't be allowed to trample everything that both of them had once believed in and walk away unscathed.

Katz's life would count for nothing in the end if it could play both ways without a day of reckoning.

For one of them, today would be that day.

He felt it in his bones, the indefinable sensation that was neither panic nor excitement, love nor hate, repulsion nor desire, a feeling that had never failed to touch him on the eve of mortal combat.

Anticipation, knowing that the game could still go either way, for life or death.

But, in the last analysis, there was more involved than raw survival. It mattered *which* side you were on, or nothing mattered. If the different sides were interchangeable, it meant that there were no such things as good and evil, right and wrong. It meant that every battle fought throughout the span of human history had been an utter waste of time.

Katz felt no need to validate his own existence after all these years, but other voices had been whispering around him since they'd all sat down at Stony Man. Lost comrades, sacrificed for causes they believed in, cut down in their prime while fighting for a nation, a religion, a political ideal.

Ignoring Auerbach would be the same as spitting on their graves.

Inside the lobby Calvin James was waiting for his comrades by the elevators, trying to be inconspicuous as they approached.

"He's gone ahead?" Katz asked.

"Two minutes, give or take."

"We'll let him have two more."

"How badly do you want this guy alive?"

"He seems to be our only hope for tracking down the hostages without a full-scale blitz."

"We're in a box if he decides to fight."

"He's not a kamikaze type," Katz said. "Have we got the stairs, as well?"

"Back there." James cocked a thumb across one shoulder toward a corridor behind him. "Mainly service, but I gather tenants use them now and then for exercise."

"We'll need to cover them."

"My treat. You want to synchronize?"

Katz checked his watch. "One minute thirty-five should do it. If you start right now, we should be close."

"I'm on my way."

"Take care."

HE'D BEEN WORRIED briefly while he waited, but the lobby call from Feldman helped him to relax. All clear, and they'd pulled it off without a hitch. Delivery on command and cash in pocket, free and clear while the police were picking over corpses on the boulevard in shantytown.

Their losses were acceptable, and none of them would lead investigators back to Auerbach or Feldman. The cartel would be suspected, certainly, but proving that suspicion was a different thing entirely. There would still be hell to pay—investigations, government commissions and the like—but it would be Costanza's job to carry out negotiations for the woman's safe release.

Assuming that he ever meant for her to walk away.

As far as Auerbach was concerned, it made no difference in the scheme of things. The woman and her brat were mere statistics, casualties of war, without intrinsic value in themselves. If they meant something to Costanza, it was his responsibility to trade them off for a strategic victory.

It had been risky sending Feldman out so soon, but Auerbach knew it was vital to preserve their image as a pair of foreign businessmen in Medellín, conducting operations with at least a modicum of common sense. The downtown office was a part of that facade, its maintenance a cover they could ill afford to cast aside. Trans-Global served a purpose but it also generated bogus paperwork, potentially incriminating in itself, which Auerbach refused to leave behind.

When it was time to go—soon now perhaps—he meant to leave a trail devoid of clues and signposts for his enemies. The empty files would take them nowhere, killing time with speculation while their quarry found new clients half a world away.

Because he recognized the risks in Medellín, he'd dispatched his junior partner to conduct the sweep. If anything went wrong, he trusted Feldman to delay the enemy while Auerbach took flight. It was a plan they had rehearsed a thousand times.

But now his friend was back safe and sound. The doorbell summoned Auerbach, and he was smiling as he turned the knob, retreating toward the well-stocked bar.

"I don't mind telling you I was concerned. I nearly telephoned."

"Why didn't you?"

It was a pointless question, but he answered, anyway. "Exposure, Chaim. You know the rules."

"Of course."

"A whiskey? Wine perhaps?"

"No thanks."

He picked up something in his partner's voice, an undertone he couldn't identify.

"Is something wrong?"

He turned in time to watch as Feldman slipped the final button on his jacket, spreading it to show a thick belt strapped around his waist.

"We need to talk," he said.

11

Bolan's second target for the day was an exclusive restaurant in El Poblado, one of the wealthiest areas of Medellín. It was owned and operated by José Mercado and was popular among *los mágicos,* the cocaine dealers, for its security arrangements, privacy and the outstanding menu, boasting chefs from Paris and New York. Aware that all his "better" customers were forced to travel with a retinue of bodyguards, Mercado had provided separate seating for the help behind a wall of mirrored glass in order to rescue all concerned from the embarrassment of having gunmen stand around outside.

Despite all that, a move against the restaurant demanded some precautionary measures on the theory that selected patrons might be innocent—or relatively so—of dealing in cocaine. He bore no animosity against the kitchen staff unless they came up shooting in the crunch, and Bolan would content himself with damage to the building if it helped to make his point.

In fact, a few survivors were essential to the plan.

He meant to send the Medellín cartel a message it couldn't ignore, concerning the abduction of a widow and her child. *Los mágicos* could buy themselves some time by freeing Dominga and Andeana Franco... or they could prepare to pay the price for their intransigence. The death of either hostage would ignite a white-hot fire, with Bolan using every means at his disposal to eradicate the enemy.

"We're here," Grimaldi announced.

Approaching on their left was Mercado's high-priced eatery, a long facade of bricks and stone with deeply tinted windows facing on the street. Assassins driving past would never pick out a special target, and Bolan reckoned the glass was bulletproof in any case. A strafing run against the restaurant would be a waste of time, but Bolan had another plan in mind.

"Let's try around in back," he said.

"Suits me."

The parking lot reminded the warrior of a showroom on Rodeo Drive. The cheapest vehicle in sight was a Mercedes, looking almost stodgy in the company of Jaguars, Porsches, Maseratis and the occasional Rolls-Royce. Their rental four-door was a hopeless loser by comparison.

"You think I'll pass?"

Grimaldi looked him over, checking out the khaki jumpsuit with its bogus name tag and the battered leather satchel on his lap.

"It isn't you," he answered.

"Fair enough. It doesn't have to be."

He reached beneath his seat and found the silenced mini-Uzi. The cargo pockets of his jumpsuit bulged with extra magazines, his satchel bearing fireworks of a different kind.

"All set," he told Grimaldi as he flicked off the submachine gun's safety. "Remember, if it takes me more than five, you're out of here."

"My watch has been a little slow all day."

"Don't give me that. You know as well as I do if I'm not outside in five, I won't be coming."

"Well—"

"I want your word."

"Okay. Just be here, will you?"

"Do my best."

He put the rental car behind him, circling around in back and moving toward the service entrance that would put him in the kitchen. The back door lookout met him coming in, a question on his lips as Bolan swung up the Uzi and stitched a burst across his chest. The guy went down without a whimper, sliding backward on the polished floor. Bolan found that he had the full attention of the kitchen staff.

"Get out!" he ordered, waving them in the direction of the exit. *"¡Vamos!"*

He didn't have to tell them twice. Bolan gave them time to reach the parking lot before he started checking out the corners, making sure no one had remained behind.

Phase one accomplished, he headed toward the double doors that featured smallish windows with a clear view of the dining areas on either side. On Bolan's left the big-league patrons took up a half-dozen tables, talking quietly among themselves, a preview of the dinner rush to come. Beyond the mirrored wall he counted fifteen *pistoleros* scarfing sandwiches and chasing them with beer or wine, their lethal luggage resting on the floor beside their chairs.

He let the mini-Uzi dangle on a strap around his neck and opened up the leather satchel, lifting out two frag grenades. With one in either hand he used his thumbs to free the safety pins and dropped them onto the floor. Then he glanced again to verify that his targets were still oblivious to their approaching fate.

From this point on timing would be everything.

He took a breath and held it, then shouldered through the door to face the gunners in their private dining room. A couple glanced up from their conversations, probably expecting service, freezing for an instant as he lobbed the two grenades and ducked back out of sight.

The double blast set hanging pots and pans in motion, clattering together like percussion instruments gone mad. Returning to the scene of carnage with the Uzi in his hands, he emptied the magazine in nearly three seconds flat, the parabellum shockers finishing a job that shrapnel had begun.

Reloading on the move, he reached inside his satchel for a smoke grenade and rushed the other dining room before his adversaries could recover from their shock. A number of them had been cut by flying glass, and all looked dazed, uncomprehending as he cleared the threshold in a combat crouch.

He lobbed the smoke grenade across the room and raked the ceiling with a burst that shattered ornate light fixtures and ripped through acoustic tiles. One of the diners had an automatic pistol in his hand, and Bolan gave him one free shot before he dropped the gunner in his tracks. The rest were stretched out prone or scrambling toward the street, and Bolan let them go.

His point had been made.

Four minutes and a fraction had passed. Grimaldi sat drumming his fingers on the steering wheel as the Executioner emerged. "All done?"

"Must be. They split without dessert."

"Tough break." Grimaldi cracked a smile. "You can't please all the people all the time."

"I SEE."

There was no need to ask about the belt Feldman wore, its armed-and-ready indicator glowing amber where the buckle ought to be. It would be plastique, Auerbach decided, with a radio control.

"About the telephone... I had no choice."

He let that pass. "Is there a microphone, as well?"

"I don't believe so. They were leery of conflicting signals with the detonator."

"Very well." He stood and waited, making Feldman work.

"They took me from the office, Isaac."

"So I gather. And Maria?"

Feldman shook his head. "She didn't see. They waited in the lobby."

"Well, that's something, anyway."

"They want the hostages."

"And me?"

A flicker, there and gone in back of Feldman's eyes. Another lie was about to wriggle free.

"They seemed to focus on the woman and her child."

"Who are they, Chaim?"

"I really couldn't say. The two who picked me up were gringos, possibly American. I also saw a black and a Hispanic—not Colombian, I think. The man in charge was definitely an Israeli. Five foot eight or nine, blue eyes, gray hair. I'd put him somewhere in his fifties. He was wearing a prosthetic arm."

Auerbach's scrotum tightened like a fist. "Which arm?"

"The right, I think." Chaim closed his eyes, remembering. "Yes, it was certainly the right."

"My God!"

"You know this man?"

"We've met."

"Who is he?"

"Never mind. The name won't tell us who he's working for, and we have more immediate concerns."

He wasted no time checking out the belt. It would be tamper-proof, if they were any good at all, and Yakov Katzenelenbogen heading up the team told Auerbach they'd be very good indeed. It also told him there would be no quarter once the battle had been joined.

"How many followed you?"

"I counted four."

There would be others, almost certainly, but Auerbach was focused on their leader now. "The one-armed man?"

Chaim nodded. "Also the Hispanic and the black. Another white man drove the car. He barely spoke, but I believe he was Canadian."

"Never mind."

He stepped behind the bar and poured himself a whiskey, this time downing it without an invitation to his partner. While he drank his free hand slid along a hidden shelf and clasped the compact automatic pistol waiting there.

Emerging from behind the bar, he had the gun in his pocket, covered by his hand.

"Let's step outside."

If Feldman was concerned about the move, he kept it to himself. The rooftop patio was spacious, with a built-in swimming pool and potted trees, brick barbecues, a panoramic view of the city.

"You tell them what they want to know?"

"It's not that simple, Chaim. You know Costanza has the hostages."

"Of course, but—"

"If we sell him out, he'll have us killed. You know that, too."

"*They'll* kill us if we don't. They're just downstairs. At least we'll have a head start with Costanza, and they might get lucky."

"Do you really think they'd let us walk away? With all of this?"

As Auerbach spoke, he gestured toward his partner with his free hand, indicating the explosive belt that Feldman wore.

"I asked them that. They said—"

"Exactly what you hoped to hear. I must say you surprise me, Chaim. This play is such an obvious attempt to kill us both. I'm really disappointed that you bought their shopworn line."

A frown of apprehension furrowed Feldman's face. "They would have blown the charge by now if that was all they wanted."

"How can they be sure we're together, Chaim?"

He drew the automatic from his pocket, stepping back another pace before he fired. Deliberately high, the bullet struck Feldman in the throat and knocked him off balance, backward, toward the swimming pool. Another round drilled him well above the belt before he toppled over with a splash.

Auerbach was sprinting for the cover of his quarters as the water shorted wires and batteries. It was a toss-up whether instantaneous immersion would deactivate the charge or set it off, but Auerbach didn't have long to wait.

The detonation jarred him off his feet, a blood-streaked geyser shooting thirty feet into the air. Concussion split the concrete bottom of the pool, and by the time the water fell again it had begun to drain away, ten thousand gallons rushing into ducts and interspaces, bulging ceilings on the floor below.

It was a problem for the janitors to cope with. Auerbach retreated toward the wall safe where he kept his travel papers and emergency supply of cash. There might be time to save himself in spite of everything.

And then he heard the sound of automatic weapons in the corridor outside.

LIGHTS FLICKERED in the elevator when the bomb went off, a tremor rippling through the walls, but it continued on its way.

"Five dollars says we lost our ace," James said.

"No bet." Katz flicked the safety off his H&K MP-5K, the others readying their weapons as the elevator leveled off on nine. He was expecting trouble when the door hissed open, but they were covering an empty plastic chair, a radio and a men's magazine beside it on the floor.

"At least we got ourselves a small diversion," James remarked.

"Let's take advantage of it while we can," Encizo said.

They stepped out of the elevator together, just in time to catch the sentry with his back turned, moving down the hall at double time. The elevator's chimes alerted him to unexpected company, and he turned back to face them, groping for a hidden pistol.

It wasn't even close.

Three streams of automatic gunfire converged and punched him off his feet, a life-size rag doll sprawling on the thick shag carpeting. Downrange, a door flew open and another sentry lurched into the hall with a shotgun in his hands.

James hit him with a zig-zag burst between the neck and knees, the slender body twitching spastically as if his feet were planted on a live high-voltage wire. As he collapsed, his finger clenched around the shotgun's trigger, squeezing off a blast that ripped the ceiling panels overhead.

Before they'd advanced ten feet a brown arm poked around the door jamb, pudgy fingers wrapped around an automatic spitting fire. They scattered, dropping prone, and Katz ripped off a burst that chewed across the plaster, ripping flesh and bone to tatters at the elbow. Encizo was up and on his way before the gunner found his voice, a short screech silenced by another point-blank burst.

The last two gunners confronted their enemies together, both firing blindly as they cleared the door. Katz heard a bullet whisper past his face, and then the MP-5K's rattle drowned the hiss of more incoming rounds. He raked the corridor from left to right, his comrades joining in to cut the gunners down.

Two doors remained, and at least one enemy alive...unless the premature explosion had obliterated Auerbach along with Feldman.

"On me," Katz growled.

They checked the open doors of two apartments, verifying that the lifeless sentries were alone. A third suite—Feldman's—was immaculate, no hint that it was occupied, aside from suits and matching luggage in the closet.

That left one.

Katz tried the knob and found it open, ducking backward as the door swung free, the sitting room revealed. Broad windows facing on the rooftop patio had shattered, littering the carpet with a sparkling layer of glass. Bright shards protruded from the walls and furniture, reminding Katz of a fakir's residence, complete with bed of pain.

When no one tried to shoot his head off, Katz went in, his submachine gun leading the way. Glass crunched underfoot and gave his every move away. Outside, the swimming pool emitted sloppy gurgling noises, like a bathtub drain, the water level dropping rapidly.

It was apparent that the bomb—and Feldman—had exploded on the patio, perhaps within the swimming pool itself. There were no visible remains of Auerbach outside or in the sitting room, but if the men had scuffled, fallen in the pool together—

"Katz."

The old, familiar voice. He swiveled toward the bedroom door, his submachine gun covering his enemy. The gun in Auerbach's fist was pointed at his chest, unwavering.

"We meet again," Auerbach said, his one eye flicking toward the door. "Why don't you introduce your friends?"

"There isn't time."

"Of course. You're in a hurry, I suppose."

"And you."

A careless shrug from Auerbach. "I think you'll find the Medellín authorities more sympathetic to my cause than yours. You've bombed my home and murdered several licensed bodyguards unless I'm very much mistaken."

"Don't forget your partner."

"No. They'll have to strain him through the ceiling tiles downstairs, I should imagine. Not much left for mama to identify."

"I want the hostages."

"Too late. The client took delivery some time ago."

"Location, then."

"My service comes complete with guarantees of confidentiality."

"Your service to Costanza's scum?"

"To paying clients, Katz. Who signs your paycheck, by the way?"

Katz clenched his teeth around a curse. "The only way you'll live to spend that money is to give us what we need."

"I haven't worked for charity in years. Perhaps if there was something you could offer me . . ."

"Your life."

"I have that now."

"Don't trust the status quo."

"And if I pull this trigger, Katz? What then?"

"You die."

"A heartbeat after you. The difference is that you'll die knowing you failed."

"Goddamn it, Auerbach!"

"Emotion. It's a weakness, I assure you. Warriors need their wits about them to survive."

"I'm curious about what happened. Why you turned."

"Who says I have? Our job was always killing off the enemy selected for us by superiors. Unquestioning, and poorly paid on top of that. I choose my enemies these days—and name my price."

"How much is that, to sell your soul?"

"I doubt you could afford me, Katz."

Katz shifted slightly, weighing angles of attack. Auerbach's eye and the muzzle of his weapon followed the Israeli commando as he moved. "We're only looking for the woman and her child."

"With Chaim wired up to detonate on impact? Don't insult me, Katz."

"Are they alive?"

"They were when I delivered them," Auerbach replied. "Of course, I haven't seen them since."

"Costanza?"

Auerbach smiled and shook his head. "I already told you, Katz. I have a code of ethics to observe."

"And what about conscience?"

"It got lost somewhere along the way. I find the enemies begin to look alike, don't you?"

"Not even close."

"You always did see things in black and white. That's a degree of blindness, I believe."

Katz saw the move in Auerbach's eye before he made it, and the Phoenix Force leader squeezed off two rounds as he lurched sideways to the floor. Auerbach fired a double punch, his bullets slicing empty air.

Katz's rounds found their target, drilling through his shirt and jacket, dropping him, the automatic spinning from his outstretched hand. He knelt beside his former comrade, hearing movement in the room behind him, willing his teammates to keep their distance.

"Now?"

The eyes swam into focus on his face, and Auerbach dredged up a crooked smile. "Why not? The ranch, Katz."

He muttered something else before he died, a whisper, nearly lost. It sounded like "Good luck."

12

"The ranch, you think?" Grimaldi asked when they were seated in the safehouse living room.

"It fits," Katz replied. "It's the safest place he has, and he can lift them out by air in nothing flat if anything goes wrong."

"What now?" James asked.

The Executioner sat back, a cup of steaming coffee in his hand, and scanned their faces. "It's no good rattling Costanza's cage," he said at last. "We've pushed him to the edge already. Any more, and he might start mailing fingers just to slow us down."

"His buddies?" Manning offered.

"Pretty much the same. From this point on they'll either play or not, depending on how strong they feel. If they sit it out, we'll have a chance to wipe them out on the rebound, if we pull it off."

"And 'it' would be...?" McCarter's tone left no doubt he knew the answer going in.

Bolan glanced at the Briton. "We'll have to hit the ranch, do what we can to get the Francos out and wrap this up before we're out of time."

"You made the recon in advance," Grimaldi said. "We're looking at defense in-depth as I recall."

The warrior nodded, sipping at his coffee. "That's affirmative. Costanza has the natives bribed or terrorized to act as lookouts, and at least a couple of the villages are armed.

On top of that he mounts professional patrols in no-man's-land, and you can look for heavy hardware on the site."

"Delightful." Manning's tone wasn't reflected in his smile.

"I'm counting on some air support," Bolan said, glancing at Grimaldi.

"I can drop you down the bastard's chimney if you want," the pilot replied.

"No thanks. We've got a better chance approaching on the ground if we can slip around Costanza's scouts. I want him covered by the time he takes it in his head to ice the hostages."

"Good luck," another voice chimed in.

Bolan glanced across the room at Charlie McPherson and his three RCMP subordinates. "You paid your way with Feldman," he informed them. "Nothing says you have to go the whole nine yards."

McPherson frowned. "We didn't volunteer and draw vacation time to come down here and watch the news on television, friend. We'd like to tag along. I can assure you we won't get in your way."

The other Mounties nodded, grinning, but there was determination in their eyes. It never crossed Mack Bolan's mind that they'd let him down deliberately. And yet . . .

"It's not the Great White North out there," he said. "What kind of jungle training do you have?"

"I'd call it slim to none," McPherson answered. "But we've done survival courses with the SAS and handled hostage situations before. We wouldn't pass for virgins."

"Fair enough. On this hike any stragglers find their own way back, alone."

"I wouldn't have it any other way."

The Executioner glanced back at Grimaldi. "Maps and aerials?"

"You bet."

The graphics were a case of mix-and-match. They had a topographic map of Medellín and the surrounding countryside, with the approximate location of surrounding villages inked in by hand. A wrinkled sheet of newsprint had the jungle trails sketched out by Father Lazaro. Half a dozen glossies, taken from the air, depicted the Costanza mansion and surrounding grounds, complete with tennis courts and riding paddocks, servants' quarters and the private zoo.

"Are those giraffes?" Grimaldi asked.

"I wouldn't be a bit surprised," Bolan replied.

"We ought to get a bonus out of this from the Humane Society."

"Don't kid yourself. Those animals are living better than the coca pickers on Costanza's payroll."

"It'd be a goddamn shame if someone let those tigers out."

"It would at that," Bolan agreed. "Okay. Let's get down and work this out. We won't get far with wheels beyond this point." His finger stabbed the topographic map along a slender thread of mountain highway. "Any farther and we'll find ourselves on a collision course with the patrols."

"On top of that," Encizo said, "we ought to save time going overland."

"Around the villages, you mean?" Bolan asked.

"We'll have to if they're working for Costanza."

"Right. This map—" Bolan pointed at the padre's sketch "—should help us there. The measurements aren't what you'd call precision work, but we can trust the source."

"Too bad we haven't got an overlay," James said.

"We'll fake it." Bolan laid the two maps side by side and started sketching in the trails. "Anywhere beyond this point, we're subject to potential contact with Costanza's first-line troops."

"One thing about these villagers," McCarter said.

"What's that?"

"They act as lookouts for Costanza, right?"

"Affirmative."

"Does that mean they patrol outside the villages, as well?"

"Unknown. We'll have to play that part of it by ear."

"And if they try to stop us?"

Bolan frowned. "I'd rather not involve civilians, but it's ultimately their decision. If they come out shooting, do your best to minimize the casualties."

"That brings to mind another point," Encizo said.

"Which is?" Bolan asked.

"F-2, the DAS—whatever. Some of them are in Costanza's pocket from the jump. I can foresee official opposition down the line."

"You all know where I stand on taking out uniforms," Bolan told them. "I'm not asking anybody else to sacrifice himself on my behalf, but if it's down to killing cops, I plan to disengage."

"We might not have a choice," the Cuban told him.

"We'll deal with that one as it comes. I'm hoping Franco's people and the crowd at the DAS are still pissed off enough to look the other way. I guess we'll see." Bolan waited, half expecting other questions or objections, but they never came. "Okay," he said at last. "Let's take a stroll around the house."

"COSTANZA."

It wasn't a question, and José Mercado understood that his companion was accusing rather than collecting information for himself. The charge made sense in many ways.

"Can you be sure?"

"Who else would profit from destroying both of us?" Rodriguez asked. "Who called for peace and used the time we gave him to recoup his losses, strengthening his own position in the field?"

"But why?"

"Because he *can*," Rodriguez said. "We helped him deal with Franco. Now he steals the widow and her child, guns down a dozen members of the DAS, and we all share the heat. He hopes it'll keep us occupied while he's busy bombing cars and restaurants.''

Mercado stiffened, angry color rising in his cheeks. Still, there were doubts he couldn't cast aside without some explanation. ''We weren't the only ones attacked,'' he said. ''Remember that. Costanza lost men, too, his training school and more. If we weren't responsible for those attacks, then who?''

''The DAS perhaps, or the Americans. Who knows? Who cares?''

''We should, if there's a possibility the same group may have come for us.''

''Costanza's our enemy,'' Rodriguez snapped. ''He murdered Lupe Vargas and the others. He destroyed your restaurant in El Poblado and humiliated both of us before the whole of Medellín.''

''If what you say is true, there can be only one response.''

''We are agreed, then.''

''But the hostages...''

''A woman and one child. Their only value lies in the publicity they generate. Tonight the government in Bogotá is seething with disgust and hatred for Costanza, but the yellow bastards are afraid to move against him. Should *we* destroy him in the meantime, I foresee a hero's welcome in the streets.''

''The captives?''

''We aren't to blame for what Costanza might have done,'' Rodriguez replied. ''No one expects to get them back alive in any case.''

''You'd kill them, then?''

''It wouldn't be the first time a woman or a child died for cocaine. First, I want Costanza's filthy head to decorate my wall at home. The rest is secondary.''

''And without Ortega to succeed him—''

"There's no one else we need to fear," Rodriguez finished for him, smiling. "We can pick and choose the members of his family we wish to use. As for the rest..."

He left it hanging, but his smile was cold, removing any doubts Mercado might have had about the fate of those who failed to make the grade.

More dead, and it had never preyed upon his mind before... until the past few days had offered him a vision of his own mortality. Despite his money and his influence, the power he could wield within Colombia and well beyond, Mercado understood that he was living in a madhouse where the lowest, most inconsequential peasant in the land might kill him, given half a chance and the incentive of a hundred-dollar fee. It made Mercado wonder, recently, if he'd chosen wisely when he picked a life-style for himself so long ago.

And then the money started whispering sweet nothings in his ear, and he forgot about his apprehension, recognizing that Luis Costanza was a threat to everyone around him. He'd never rest until he had it all, the whole damn country for himself, and a monopoly on the product.

Left alone Costanza would devour all of them in time. And when he thought about the past eight days, Mercado had a feeling that the time was now. "It won't be easy," he remarked.

"You'll join me, then?"

"We must defend ourselves."

And afterward, he thought, Rodriguez would bear watching.

It was the nature of cocaine that dealers double-crossed each other constantly without a second thought beyond the odds of getting burned. With profits so outrageous treachery became a daily fact of life, betrayal and assassination practiced as basic tools of the trade.

How many times before he'd reached the apex of his calling had Mercado taken part in burns and rip-offs, killing hapless runners for the merchandise they carried,

building up a stockpile of his own? Too many times for him
to count with any certainty.

This time, he thought, the action they'd be taking would
be self-defense, a perfectly legitimate response to threats
against their lives, the empires they'd built from scratch.

In retrospect it had been foolish to support Costanza's
plan of all-out war against the government. No matter that
the dealers virtually held the purse strings in Colombia,
maintaining private armies larger than the DAS and better
armed than many units of the national forces. Traffic in
cocaine was supposed to be a "secret" occupation, even
when the dealers threw their cash around and squabbled
over territory, spilling blood. Police and judges, legislators
and accomplices in every walk of life preserved their "innocence" by pointing out that crimes remained unsolved,
the perpetrators unidentified.

Until Costanza grew so arrogant that he'd run for congress, buying the election, publicly proclaiming that cocaine was a blessing for Colombia, a chance to make their
homeland great. Costanza craved the spotlight in his every
word and deed, but the publicity he courted was destroying
all of them.

Publicity meant widespread indignation, movements toward reform. And stripped of all its platitudes reform meant
wiping out cocaine as a source of income and corruption. It
meant crushing the cartel.

Displeased by the reaction he'd brought upon himself—
upon them all—Costanza struck out like a spoiled brat
throwing temper tantrums. If the government and people of
Colombia refused to see things his way, they'd be destroyed. Outspoken critics of the drug cartel were slaughtered left and right, regardless of their government positions
or their standing in society. If editorials were published
calling for an end to bloodshed, well, it was a simple thing
to dynamite a newspaper office with everyone inside.

But somewhere in the midst of all the death and suffering the point was lost upon José Mercado.

At the outset of Costanza's war against the world, Mercado had regarded it as daring, even brilliant—a technique that would humiliate the hypocrites in government and bring them to their knees. In fact, it took a number of them to their graves, but others always took the place of martyred victims.

And the war went on—five years, then seven, creeping up on ten with no end yet in sight. They had eliminated hundreds of officials, thousands of civilians, and they hadn't gained an inch of ground. It was a fact that profits from cocaine had increased each quarter, but beyond a certain point the chase became an abstract concept, nearly meaningless. In millions it had been impressive, rolling off the tongue like something special. Now, in billions, there were dollars socked away in countless banks that none of them would ever see, much less enjoy. Their great-great-grandchildren could live in style by raking off the interest from those bank accounts, and *they* would never see the principal.

Sometimes Mercado thought that being fabulously rich was similar to claiming ownership of the entire planet. Around the globe he knew there were things to see, delicious foods to sample, lovely women anxious for a chance to warm his bed...and if he lived to be a thousand, he'd never have the time to taste a fraction of the pleasures that awaited him. Especially while Costanza's godforsaken ego war required them all to live in hiding like a band of fugitives within their native land.

The time had come for logic to assert itself and take control.

"It won't be easy," he repeated, speaking almost to himself.

"By land perhaps," Rodriguez said. "But from the air..."

THE NEWS of Auerbach and Feldman struck Costanza hard. The dead men weren't friends, by any means, but he re-

spected them within his limitations, and he had planned to
rely on them for protection in the troubled days to come.

No doubt about it, things would soon be getting worse in
Medellín.

Costanza's enemies refused to learn from their mistakes;
regardless of the price they paid in blood. They were determined to destroy him and everything he'd worked for
through the years . . . but they wouldn't succeed.

He had the woman and her child. In Bogotá the president
and his advisers knew Luis Costanza as someone you could
trust to keep his word where murder was concerned. If he
informed them that the woman and her brat would die at
noon tomorrow, if the animals responsible for causing him
to suffer such indignities weren't identified and brought to
heel, they knew Costanza meant exactly what he said.

The final question was whether they'd play along . . . or
whether they possessed the information he required.

He wouldn't contemplate the possibility of failure now
that he had come this far. Costanza had accumulated wealth
and power beyond the wildest dreams of common men, en-
abling him to deal with hostile governments as if he had a
private country of his own.

Which, in effect, he had.

Colombia had sold herself, to a degree, and he was picking up the tab. Each man and woman had a price somewhere between the trivial and the ridiculous. Where
politicians cherished an inflated vision of themselves, it was
Costanza's job to introduce reality. No member of the team
was irreplaceable, except its leader, and he meant to hold the
reins at any cost.

Benito Franco had been one of those idealists who stubbornly refused to play the game. So be it. He was gone, and
now the remnants of his family would be useful to Costanza in the final stages of his war.

And it would have to be the final stage, he realized.

The years of urban combat had already cost Colombia
too much in terms of national respect and credibility,

goodwill among the other nations of the world. Costanza knew about such things, and while his chief concerns were always personal, he harbored no desire to see his native land disgraced, impoverished and finally destroyed.

Cocaine was the answer to a prayer, and he'd used it wisely up to now, a product that would make him rich while bending venal politicians to his every whim. Because Costanza knew the end from the beginning and decided what was beneficial for Colombia, his power molded minds and votes in Bogotá. A member of the legislature in his own right, he had been riding high until the recent troubles had broken around his head. First Franco, then the nameless enemies who had chipped their way around the fringes of his empire, opening fresh wounds to let his reputation bleed away.

The day of reckoning had come when he would deal with *all* his enemies together, purging them with fire and steel. As soon as he identified the men responsible for threatening his way of life, he'd destroy them, root and branch. Their family trees would be uprooted, hacked to pieces, cast into the fire.

No man or group of men would stand before Costanza in his rage.

As for his "allies," they could stand and fight or run for cover like the cowards they were. His treaty with Mercado and Rodriguez was a matter of convenience at the moment, freeing troops and guns from one front to be used against a different, more important enemy. Costanza didn't overlook the possibility that his new "friends" might plot against him, but he was ready for them if they tried. His spies were everywhere. One word, and both of them would simply disappear.

Unless . . .

He scowled and pushed the vague, distracting thoughts away. Mercado and Rodriguez were a sideshow. There was little—make that nothing—either one of them could do to harm him now. Secure inside his fortress, with his hostages, Costanza would negotiate from strength. If Bogotá decided the woman and her child weren't enough, their deaths acceptable if they would bring Costanza down...well, he'd have to brief the liberal press on their response.

What men the elected officials were! Costanza thought. The only time that most of them displayed a trace of energy was when they scrambled for their payoffs...or amused themselves with whores provided by the cartel. Most of the bedroom sessions had been taped against the day when this or that official took his holier-than-thou approach too seriously in the legislative halls.

Survival was an instinct born in every living creature, but a man who trusted instinct on its own would soon be ancient history. Beyond the primal impulse, coming out on top took planning and initiative, the keen ability to see through bogus "friends" and recognize potential enemies on sight.

And, when you made your living from cocaine, the potential enemies were everywhere, true friends few and far between.

Costanza was content, for now, to let his enemies believe he was on the ropes. If they perceived him as a desperate man, prepared to throw his life away on futile gestures, they might let their own guard down enough for him to strike a telling blow. The quickest way to die in any war was nurturing a sense of overconfidence.

But first he had to play the waiting game.

His bait was tethered, and the snares were all in place. Costanza's prey would be along in time because they had no choice. Defending worthless peasants was a fatal weakness of the law-abiding class. Costanza had seen grown men throw their lives away to help a stranger they'd never seen before, and never would again.

It was a travesty of common sense that he could use to his advantage in the hours ahead.

As he destroyed his adversaries one by one.

13

Sergeant Charlie McPherson of the RCMP paused to wipe his sweaty face and shift his pack, relieving pressure of the canvas straps across his aching shoulders. Dusk or not, despite the altitude, the forest seemed intent on suffocating him. If he survived the night, McPherson reckoned he'd have lost at least ten pounds.

If he survived.

The tall American who called himself Mike McKay had made it clear about their odds, with ten men on the ground against a private army that included scores—or even hundreds—of ambitious guns. On top of that the natives were expected to be hostile, informing Costanza of the arrival of intruders, maybe even wading in to fight if they felt so inclined.

A simple nature walk, and it would be a bloody miracle if *any* of their strike force saw the sun come up tomorrow.

Still, they had commitment on their side, and military hardware that would do the job all right...if they were given half a chance. They also had surprise, to start—unless they ran into those villagers, or one of the patrols Costanza mounted day and night around his fortress home.

McPherson's men were young, unmarried volunteers. He couldn't vouch for any one of them as far as social graces were concerned, but they were doggedly committed to their goal of breaking the cartel...or shaking it at any rate.

Surrounded by the forest now, a full half hour since they'd left their jeeps and started overland on foot, it crossed McPherson's mind that he'd be responsible for anything that happened to his men tonight. He'd recruited them himself, selecting from a list of several dozen applicants and swearing them to secrecy before he'd sketched the briefest outline of the mission they were called on to perform. Once he'd been briefed, each finalist had been told he could walk away and there would be no hard feelings.

And none of them had walked.

In retrospect it was a shitty deal for all concerned. His men had drawn vacation time, which wouldn't be replaced until the normal cycle of a year had passed, and they were traveling outside their jurisdiction, out of uniform, without authority of any kind. They'd be armed, for self-defense and any other problems that arose, but an arrest on weapons charges in Colombia would be the end of it, beginning with an instant disavowal by the Canadian government.

In fact, McPherson had told them that being jailed wasn't what they should fear. If they accepted the illegal mission, they'd be opposing some of the most ruthless and sadistic narcobarons in the world, and on their own home turf. The police and judges, legislators and executives, were almost universally corrupt or frightened for their lives, unable or unwilling to resist the power of the drug cartel.

Within that atmosphere the Mounties had a secret brief to find the cocaine river's source and "use initiative" in damming the flow. If they could halt one shipment, fine. If they could prompt a shakeup in the leadership of the cartel, so much the better.

But Luis Costanza was the key.

If any of McPherson's fresh-faced troopers viewed the job as suicide, it didn't show. They knew the risks and took them on, apparently without a second thought.

And if they died tonight, McPherson knew he'd never sleep again without those bright-eyed faces coming back to haunt his dreams.

Relax, he told himself. Don't borrow trouble. By the time the cartel gunners picked them off, he'd probably be dead himself.

Oh, yeah?

He caught himself before the words escaped and glanced back to make certain his men were still behind him, hanging tough. Their tiger-stripe fatigues were dark with perspiration, but they showed no evidence of terminal fatigue.

Ahead of them, invisible in shadow, Mike McKay had signaled for a halt. The word came back in whispers, telling of a mountain river they would have to cross before they could proceed.

McPherson cracked a broad grin and called his men around. "Cinch up your undies, guys," he said. "We're going for a swim."

THE CURRENT WASN'T swift, but the water was knee-deep at the bank with slick stones underfoot, a problem if some member of the party lost it halfway over and was swept downstream. The altitude protected them from water snakes and alligators, but a drowning added up to death as surely as a gnashing set of prehistoric jaws.

They needed rope to make the crossing safely—which, in turn, meant one man crossing on his own and unsecured in order to pave the way.

"I'm up," Bolan said, sounding casual. "With fifty, sixty feet of line we should be set."

The river looked to be no more than thirty feet across, but saplings nearest to the bank were relatively weak, their roots potentially unstable in a bed of mud and clay. The extra slack would let them tie off on substantial trees some distance from the crumbling bank.

But first he had to take the rope across.

As a precaution, Bolan tied one end around his waist. The rope would trail behind him as he crossed, and if he took an unexpected header into the water, the line would let them reel him back.

In theory, anyway.

The Executioner knew from personal experience that injury and shock accelerated drowning deaths, and there were times you simply couldn't haul a body in against the current's undertow. Worse yet was the possibility of being strafed by hostile snipers as he reached midstream, a sitting target with nowhere to run or hide, and damn little to offer in the way of self-defense.

"All set?"

The question came from Calvin James, and Bolan nodded in response. He took his first step off the bank, heels skidding in the moss and mud before he sank in to his knees. The water's unexpected chill took Bolan's breath away.

Slowly he forged a path across the stream, eyes fixed on the shore directly opposite. It did no good to watch his feet; he couldn't see them, anyway, and staring down would only compromise his balance when he needed it the most.

As Bolan moved across, he tested each and every step, dislodging awkward stones by feel when they appeared to be a hazard, kicking them away. Emerging on the other side, his dripping legs felt even colder on exposure to air. Retreating toward a tree he knew would serve their purpose as an anchor, Bolan nearly stumbled, cursing as he paused and tried to get his land legs back.

But it wasn't his legs that were at fault.

The ground was trembling, giving off a distant rumble that was barely audible.

More seismic action in the mountain range, he thought. Costanza's "tame" volcano? Overhead, a screeching flight of birds scattered in the night.

Ignoring them, he tied the rope off, tested it with all his weight and doubled back to let the others know he was finished. They'd use a slipknot on the west bank to allow retrieval of the rope when all had safely crossed.

Katz went first, the CAR-15 clasped in his good left hand, his prosthetic locked around the guide line as he waded. Two down and eight to go.

The Executioner stood back and waited for his team to reassemble on the shore.

A FEW MILES DISTANT Father Julio Lazaro felt the tremors in his church and listened to the stone walls creaking like an old man's bones. He crossed himself and walked outside to greet the coming darkness, breathing warm air after the prevailing chill inside.

He'd been praying for the tall American and his companions when the earth began to move. They were abroad tonight, preparing for a confrontation with Costanza's army, and the priest wished them well. Some would have said it wasn't his place, a man of God, to root for one side or the other in a private war, but he'd seen enough of the indignity Costanza heaped upon his fellow man to recognize an evil blight made flesh.

Father Lazaro couldn't claim to know the men arrayed against Costanza. He'd met with two of them, and spoken with the tall American at length, but the rest were strangers to him. Still, he knew within his heart that they weren't Costanza's competition, dealers in cocaine who desired Costanza's death for private gain. They were crusaders in the true sense of the word, and if a priest wasn't allowed to offer prayers on the behalf of those who did God's work—regardless of their tools—then it was possible he'd been mistaken in his calling.

He didn't know their plans, or the specific hour of attack, but he had spies in Medellín and the surrounding countryside. They told him of a caravan—three jeeps, ten men and their equipment—proceeding north from town on narrow forest trails. The jeeps would be abandoned soon, from logic and necessity, while they continued on their way by foot.

And was Costanza waiting for them? Did the spider feel an oh-so-gentle tugging at the long strands of his web?

The priest prayed Costanza's nerve and troops would fail him in the coming fight. A squad of ten appeared to have no chance against the overwhelming odds, but there was always hope. Years of living hand-to-mouth and praying for his people to survive had taught Lazaro that.

In life there was at least the seed of hope for better days.

He studied the volcano, darkness foiling his attempt to see if there were wisps of smoke emerging from the ancient cone. There had been smoke that afternoon in quantities, but it had died away toward dusk, as if the grumbling mountain felt a need for sleep.

And now the sleeper stirred.

Lazaro could remember childhood days in Antioquia Province when he believed the smoking mountain and its hot springs were the concrete evidence of hell below. Why else would smoke and steaming water rise from underground when simple stone and earth were plainly cool? Some afternoons he'd wandered near the hot springs, kneeling to press one ear against the earth and listen for the wailing sounds of tortured souls. The net result had been a dirty ear and disillusionment when Father Esperanza set him straight.

Tonight, beneath the stars, the priest half believed in hell again. Long years of service to the church had more or less persuaded him that hell was just a euphemism for man's daily life, but if there *was* a roiling lake of fire somewhere below his feet, reserved for evil souls . . . Father Lazaro had some brand-new candidates in mind.

It went against his training, but the priest despised Luis Costanza for the misery cocaine brought to countless other souls around the world. Despite the daily headlines from America, its greatest impact was experienced in Medellín and the surrounding countryside where villagers Lazaro knew from childhood were compelled to trade their lives and souls for pocket money, struggling to feed their families on the profits from cocaine in a society that offered nothing better.

And the priest was ashamed that he'd done no more to stop the traffickers in recent years.

Unconsciously he flexed his hands inside their bandages, the pain of open wounds reminding him of one occasion when he crossed Costanza's path. The nail holes marked him like stigmata, but the priest drew no comfort from the rude comparison with Christ.

His Lord had driven moneylenders from the temple, while Lazaro stood and watched drug dealers eat his native country alive. Christ died to rescue men, while Father Julio escaped with momentary pain and brief embarrassment. Unlike the Savior, he was anxious to survive.

But he was running out of time, regardless.

The physicians were agreed on that, although they squabbled over the number of weeks and months remaining. In the end, days made no difference to a man who feared he'd lost the most important battle of his life.

Lazaro's church superiors would never have approved cooperation with the tall American to bring Costanza down...but, then again, Lazaro knew that some of them accepted donations from Costanza and his ilk, all smiles as tainted money crossed their palms. Some of them hastened to forgive the murderers of children for their crimes against humanity, dispensing absolution like a dash of after-shave.

He didn't blame the church, per se—no more than he could blame the press, police force or the legislature. Every institution in the land relied on mortal men to carry out its policies, and mortal men were fallible. They yielded to temptations of the flesh and fell for arguments like the Costanza patriotic line—cocaine as heaven's gift to an impoverished culture in Colombia.

Lazaro clenched his fists and grimaced at the pain, dismissing it.

Out there, concealed by darkness and the forest, fighting men were on their way to face Costanza's legion in a battle to the death, perhaps relying on maps and sketches he'd given to the American. If so, Lazaro might at least pretend to have an active role in what was happening.

It was the best he could do unless...

His mind made up, the priest turned and walked back to his church.

To pray.

THE VIPER SEEMED to come from nowhere, striking from a branch that Calvin James had brushed aside to clear the narrow trail. He heard a warning hiss and flinched, felt something graze his cheek before it slapped against his left shoulder. He stepped backward and took the serpent with him. It slithered across his chest, its curved fangs buried in the canvas pouch that held his first-aid kit.

"God*damn* it!"

Gary Manning reached him first, a knife blade flashing as he took the snake's head off with a single stroke and pitched the flaccid body into the darkness. James took his time about the head, his fingers smeared with blood and venom by the time he worked it free.

"I owe you one," he said.

"No sweat." Manning grinned as he added, "One thing you should think about is changing your cologne."

"So funny I forgot to laugh."

They were in hostile territory now, according to the maps. Of course, the whole country had been hostile territory from the moment they'd landed. Even so, inhabitants of Medellín put on a show of leading normal lives, conducting business, going home to families after work. Out here the rules of so-called civilized society had simply never taken hold.

Like certain neighborhoods James knew about back home.

Another rumbling, and a tremor passed beneath his feet. James couldn't tell if it was stronger this time, but it was the second time the earth had moved in the past hour. His knowledge of geology was slim to none, but it didn't require a genius to connect the tremors with the brooding cone of a nearby volcano.

He thought of Mount Saint Helens, the destruction pictured in contemporary videos, and imagined trying to fight a battle under those conditions.

In his mind James knew the mountain had undoubtedly been rumbling for decades—possibly for centuries—without a major blowup. Right now the team had more to be concerned about from restless natives and Costanza's mercenary troops than from a pool of magma simmering a mile below the surface of the earth.

They'd been hiking overland for almost an hour, and they were drawing closer to the point where mountain villages had been co-opted as an early-warning system for Costanza and his men. James didn't know if there were sentries posted near the villages, or if their hand-drawn maps were accurate enough to see them through. Regardless, there would be no turning back.

He didn't relish contact with the villagers. The vast majority drew wages from Costanza for the grunt work that maintained his transportation routes and coca labs, but James couldn't begrudge the Indians their daily bread. If some of them had graduated to the rank of overseer or paid assassin, they'd made their choice to run with jackals and accept the risks involved.

And if it came to opposition from the villagers at large, a battle for the trail, what would he do?

His duty, right.

Costanza was the target, a malignant evil threatening Colombia and the United States through his involvement with cocaine. If armed civilians took the dealer's part and tried to stop the team from getting through, there could be only one response.

Up front the point men carried automatic weapons fitted with silencers in case they made an early contact on the trail. There was no point in raising hell before the main event if another way could be found. And if his life was threatened in the jungle, in the dark, James was ready to defend himself with everything he had.

They met the ambush moments later, signaled by a verbal challenge from the darkness. James hit a combat crouch and searched the tree line for a target he could fix on, anything to give his M-16 direction in the night. No sound of firing was audible yet, but it was bound to come when Encizo ran out of soothing words.

He singled out a vaguely man-shaped silhouette and fixed his sights around chest level. It was probably a tree trunk, but at least he wasn't groping like a blind man in a maze. If things got hairy, wasting a half-dozen rounds on bark and pulp would be the least of James's problems.

He was locked and loaded, with his finger on the trigger, when the word came back from Bolan, passed along from man to man.

"Stand down. We're going in."

In *where?*

No matter. James had his orders, and he knew enough to trust the big guy's judgment in a crunch. Wherever they were going, it was Bolan's choice—and they could always start the fireworks later if the play went bad.

James passed the word along and rose from his fighting crouch. Ahead of him the troops were moving out.

He kept a finger on the trigger as he followed close behind.

THE AMBUSH could have been a killer, Bolan realized. The natives knew their turf and staked it out like expert hunters, waiting silently for game to come their way. Not many of them, granted—and their firearms would be rated obsolete by any modern army in the world—but half a dozen well-placed shots would have reduced his team by half. Worse yet, the racket—or a hasty message on the compact walkie-talkie that their leader carried—would have brought Costanza's hunters in to finish off the job.

The warning call took Bolan by surprise, as much because the trackers didn't fire, as from the fact that he was suddenly surrounded on the trail. His first reaction was to spray the tree line with his CAR-15, but common sense prevented him. If they were being warned instead of shot, the sentries must have reasons of their own.

He didn't recognize the voice at once, distorted as it was by nerves on both side of the firing line.

Beside him Rafael Encizo said, "They want to talk, and ask us not to shoot."

"I'm listening."

A moment later a short man armed with an M-1 Garand stepped from the shadows. It took another heartbeat, but his cautious smile clicked home in Bolan's mind.

He was the father of a boy who had been caught in the crossfire during Bolan's recent strike against one of Costanza's caravans. The warrior had delivered the boy to safety and the word of the American's act of kindness had spread throughout the village.

The man stepped forward, offering his hand. *"Amigo."* Friend.

The Executioner shook hands, relieved as other wraithlike figures showed themselves, their rifles angled skyward now.

"How's your son?"

"Much better, thanks to you."

"I'm glad. We have no business with your village if you'll let us pass."

The peasant frowned and said, "That won't be possible, *señor.*"

"Why's that?"

"Costanza's men have doubled their patrols beyond this point. The smallest trails are closely guarded now. Your men would all be killed within another mile."

"We'll have to take that chance."

"And waste your lives? There's a better way."

"Which is?"

"Come back with us to our village. There, I'll show you how to find Costanza, even with his army on alert."

"We haven't got a lot of time to spare," the Executioner replied. "Why can't you show us here?"

"The *traficantes* might patrol this way. We're safe inside the village."

The warrior thought about it for a moment, made his choice and nodded, turning to McCarter on his left. "Relay the word. Stand down. We're going in."

And so the word was passed along.

The trek consumed a precious quarter hour, but at least the village lay ahead of them, and more or less in the direction they were traveling. A few armed men were waiting on the outskirts, but their wives and children had been tucked away, securely out of sight.

Their host was named Fernando, and his face provided Bolan with a glimpse of how Miguel would look a few years down the road, assuming he lived to reach the ripe old age of twenty-five or so. All business now that they were "safe," Fernando knelt and used a knife to sketch a crude map in the dirt, illuminated by a hooded flashlight's beam.

"Trails here and here," he said, approximating the Lazaro sketch. "Both guarded. The canyon here isn't so easy, but the guards will stay away, I think."

"You *think?*"

Fernando shrugged and smiled again. "More chance of passing here than on the trails they watch." He traced the canyon with his blade and drew an X. "Costanza here. Six, seven miles away."

"No trail?" Encizo asked.

The man shook his head. "The animals, they go this way, but there's nothing marked for men."

"That's all we need," James said. "Get lost along the way and blow our schedule, maybe stumble into one of the patrols we're trying to avoid."

"No danger," their host told him. "I'm your guide."

A frown creased Bolan's face. "You've helped enough. You have people who depend on you right here."

"I think, perhaps, their lives and happiness depend on your success, amigo. I'll show you how to find Costanza."

"Strictly noncombatant?"

"As you wish," Fernando agreed.

Reluctant as he was to have civilians join their private battle, Bolan understood Fernando's stake in what went down. His people had been carrying Costanza's weight for years on end. Some would have said they had nothing more to lose.

Except their lives.

"All right," the warrior said at last. "We're wasting time. Let's move."

14

Fernando had advised them there would be no trail, as such, and he wasn't mistaken. Moving slowly through the darkness, Bolan watched their guide apply his keen machete to the hanging vines and clinging undergrowth that nearly blocked a narrow track carved out by forest animals in flight. He seemed to make enough noise that could allow their enemies to track them from a mile away, but if Fernando was concerned, it didn't show.

And Bolan kept his finger on the trigger of his automatic rifle all the same.

Six or seven miles remained until they reached their goal. It would have been a slightly shorter distance on the trail depicted by Lazaro's map, but fighting through an ambush was a task he wanted to avoid. They only had Fernando's guess that no one had been sent to guard the canyon they were looking for, but any odds were better than a certain brush with death.

Behind him Encizo and McCarter were the next in line, with James and Manning close behind. McPherson and his Mounties followed Manning, single-file, with Katz bringing up the rear. If anything went sour on the march, Katz had the strength and nerve to watch out for the new men on the team, preventing a necessary fallback from degenerating into chaos.

Up ahead Fernando hesitated, Bolan freezing on his heels. Mute signals brought the column to a halt without a spoken word. As the Executioner watched, Fernando swung the flat of his machete down and forward, followed by a squealing, crashing sound as something scurried for its life. The villager shrugged and cracked a brilliant smile before turning back to the trail.

It took them half an hour to reach the canyon, moving downhill all the way. The strain on Bolan's ankles was increasing with the slope, and twice he braced himself against the sound of boot heels losing purchase on the track behind him, bodies sliding through the undergrowth before they caught a vine or overhanging branch. Another klick or so, the way the ground was dropping off, and they'd have to climb hand over hand.

As if on cue, Fernando signaled for a halt and slipped his long machete back inside its sheath. Distant trees were etched in silhouette against the velvet sky, but there was nothing in between.

The canyon lay before them, carved by rushing water in another era. Below and far away an unseen river whispered over rocks that would themselves be worn away a thousand years from now.

"Down there?" McCarter asked, his tone betraying no great enthusiasm for the climb.

Fernando nodded. "The bottom here, some ninety yards. Farther on, two hundred, maybe more."

"And this route leads us to Costanza's door?"

"Yes."

James was standing on the brink and staring down at mottled darkness. "Anybody bring a parachute?" he asked.

"An easy climb," Fernando answered. "Many times the women of my village hunt for manioc below."

"Too bad we didn't bring a few of them along."

"Make sure you double-check the knots," Bolan said, handing off his coil of rope to Manning as he spoke.

Four coils should have done it, but they added a fifth for safety's sake in case Fernando had his math confused. When each and every one of them had thrown his weight against the double knots, McCarter looped one end around a sturdy tree—no slipknots here—and Manning hurled the free end into space.

It seemed to fall forever, squirming out of sight and thrashing into the ferns below. If nothing else, the noise would startle any rats or snakes that lived among the rocks and urge them out of striking range before the first man started down.

And if Fernando had it wrong about the canyon being free of gunners, they were announcing their approach in no uncertain terms.

Too late.

They'd already come this far, and it would cost them too much time to double back and find the open trail again.

"I go," Fernando offered, picking up the rope and stepping toward the precipice, his M-1 slung across his shoulders with the muzzle down.

"Hold on."

Their guide reluctantly gave up the line to Bolan and stepped back.

"You follow me," the Executioner instructed.

"Okay, if you prefer."

The warrior let him think it was raw machismo talking, but he had another motive. If there were gunners waiting in the dark below, they might be able to subdue Fernando silently, the next man falling prey without an opportunity to save himself. With Bolan on the line and braced for anything, at least the others had a chance of being warned before all hell broke loose.

"You'll hear me if I need you," Bolan said to James.

"Affirmative."

And taking up the nylon rope, he pushed off into space.

AS THE LAST MAN DOWN, Katz had a chance to watch and follow each in turn as they descended, fading out of sight. The undergrowth and darkness covered them before they traveled forty yards, less than half the distance estimated by their guide. It was an eerie feeling, standing on the precipice and watching people disappear, but he was confident there would have been a warning by now if there had been a problem.

In fact, the climb was easier than he'd imagined. There were countless toeholds weathered in the stone to give him purchase, as well as twisted roots and wiry saplings all around him when he paused to shift his grip on the rope. Instead of running over ninety yards, Katz suspected it was less. In barely fifteen minutes he was on the ground.

"If somebody finds the rope," James said, "we got a problem."

"Let it go," Katz told him. "By the time they get around to looking for it here, we'll all be having coffee back in Medellín."

"You wish."

The slope was kinder to Katz's ankles now than in the last half hour of their march. They traveled with the river on their right, spray dashing over stones in places, covering the noise of their progress to some degree. A silent forest hike was difficult enough in daylight, and the darkness made it virtually impossible. Katz blessed the river for its sound effects and hoped it would take them all the way.

He almost got his wish.

The snipers met them fifteen hundred yards below the point where they descended to the canyon floor, a pair of rifles winking from the darkness. Before the echo of the shots reached Katz's ears, he saw one of the Mounties stumble and pitch forward on his face, his weapon skittering across the stones. A cry of pain arose from somewhere in the middle of the column, and he knew exactly what was happening.

Katz went to ground behind a rugged boulder, cursing as he banged an elbow on the stone. He saw and heard the others scrambling for cover as the sound of gunfire rattled back and forth between the canyon walls.

How many guns? He was aware of two, but there could easily be more concealed among the trees and stony crags.

And then again, two snipers would be more than adequate to block the canyon if they knew their jobs.

These did.

They used their ammunition sparingly, instead of spraying lead at random in the hope of striking flesh by accident. From where he lay, Katz couldn't spot the member of their team whose painful cry accompanied the first two shots, but he could see the prostrate Mountie well enough. He wasn't moving, and the awkward angle of his limbs told Katz he would never move again.

One down at least. Their striking force reduced by ten percent.

He caught a profile of McPherson, checking out his man from a respectful distance, and the gruff Israeli knew what he was going through. It wasn't easy, leading men to meet their deaths, and some commanders never got around the shock. McPherson seemed like a survivor, but you never knew until the chips were down.

Like now.

Up front somebody made a move, both snipers blasting at him in the darkness. Katz took advantage of the brief diversion, rolling to his left and breaking for the rocky bank with loping strides. He burrowed into cover there before the nearest sniper swung around to bring him under fire. They were on more equal footing now.

He took his time, advancing through the undergrowth one short step at a time. The slightest noise would finish him—a snapping branch, a rock slide to betray his presence and provide the sniper with a target.

How far?

His point of reference was a muzzle-flash, the distance estimated as he ran for cover, and he made it something close to eighty yards. Not far, but it could take forever in the darkness, creeping over unfamiliar ground to find an enemy who should be changing his position even now.

So far the members of his squad had been returning fire reluctantly, a short burst here and there, with some of that from silenced weapons. Even so, the sounds of combat would be audible for miles. Katz wondered how the canyon would distort those sounds, deceiving listeners and—hopefully—delaying their response. Would the reports be audible to sentries at Costanza's ranch?

Too far away.

He hoped.

Katz knew the gunner should have moved, and he corrected for the shift. It would be foolish—even suicidal—for the sniper to descend and thus reduce the range between his targets and himself. A wise man would be climbing to seek a better vantage point and catch his creeping enemy off guard.

Katz climbed, twice freezing as a loose stone clattered from underneath his boots. There was no probing fire, but he'd never know if he was spotted until the first round struck him, blowing him away.

Then the sniper fired again, at Bolan and the others, giving Katz his fix. They must be on the move if his opponent had to risk exposure in the last extreme. Good thinking; he'd have to shake somebody's hand when it was done.

He glimpsed the sniper as an outline, sighting down the barrel of his weapon, and the outline was enough. Katz barely took the time to aim his CAR-15, the weapon ripping off a dozen rounds on autofire almost before a conscious plan took shape.

The Israeli saw and heard the bullets strike their mark, the sniper twitching as he lost his balance, plunging headfirst down the slope. Before he reached the bottom someone with a silenced weapon hit him with another burst to guarantee he wouldn't be getting up again.

One down, the other enemy beyond his reach unless he got off a lucky shot.

Katz shifted in the darkness, looking for a muzzle-flash, and settled down to wait.

SERGEANT MCPHERSON pulled his gaze away from the un-moving form of Corporal Michael Trask and concentrated on revenge. One sniper survived, and he was on the wrong side of the river, feeling safe and cocky with the water in between them. McPherson wondered if the shooters were equipped with radios, and whether they'd beamed a May-day before they'd opened fire.

Were reinforcements racing through the jungle to sur-round them?

No time to waste.

The river was a mystery. McPherson didn't have a clue about its depth or currents, other than the fact that it was moving swiftly through a field of boulders on his right. The giant stones would give him cover when he made his move, but if he lost his footing in the undertow, he could be swept away.

Too bad.

The river was a risk, but sitting still and waiting for Cos-tanza's cavalry was certain death. One of his men had died already, and he had others to think about, not to mention the other members of the team. McKay and his comman-dos had agreed to let the Mounties tag along, and it was time for him to get some mileage out of the commando training he'd bragged about when they were safe and warm in Medellín.

The sniper missed him coming out, a ricochet exploding into bits of stone that stung McPherson's cheek. Another round was fired before he cleared the bank, falling short, and then he hit the water running, almost going down on hands and knees before he reached the nearest boulder and ducked out of sight.

From that point on his options were distinctly limited. The sniper knew he could only move in one of two direc-tions—falling back, or pushing on to reach the next large rock in line. Whichever way he chose, a bullet would be waiting for him, and McPherson cursed himself as seven kinds of fool for acting hastily and pissing off his only chance.

A handful of the others had begun to fire on his adversary, buying time, distracting him, and the sergeant took advantage of the moment, lunging for the next stop on his dead-end run.

Halfway across, McPherson hesitated, bracing for the next run, waiting for the cover fire to pin down his adversary. Three rushes under fire left him panting by the time he reached the other bank, a stand of trees concealing him at last.

Bolan and the rest of the team broke off firing as McPherson cleared the river, saving ammunition and reducing the amount of noise that could—for all they knew—be drawing enemies from miles away. The RCMP officer began to work his way up the slope with all deliberate speed, avoiding deadfalls where he could. He knew the sniper would be moving, too, and there was no way to anticipate where the man would surface next.

The gravel saved him, rattling down from overhead. McPherson ducked backward as a single round burned past his face. He triggered off a searching burst without a hope in hell of bagging anything, then doubled back before the sniper had a chance to fire again.

This time McPherson saw the muzzle-flash and burned up half a magazine in answer, locking on the clump of ferns that screened his adversary from the naked eye. No grunt or scream signified a hit, but moments later he could hear the sniper coming down head over heels.

The body lodged against a boulder several paces to McPherson's left, and he approached with caution, wary of a trap. In fact, the guy was dead, with half a dozen solid hits between the waist and collarbone, a portion of his lower jaw ripped free and balanced on his shoulder like a grisly epaulet.

A life in recompense for Trask's, but it wasn't enough.

Retreating down the slope, McPherson knew the score was still unbalanced in Costanza's favor.

Hell, it wasn't even close.

THEY GATHERED at the river briefly, but their faces would have made a gospel singer's blood run cold. One man was dead, and three more—Fernando, Manning, James—had suffered minor flesh wounds in the fierce exchange. Mack Bolan waited while their wounds were bathed and bound, aware they were running out of time.

"What now?" McCarter asked.

"We've got no choice. Retreating's not an option," Bolan answered. "If they heard us—and it's safe to bet that *someone* did—the only bright spot is that they're above us now. They'll have to make a climb before they pick us up and even then it won't be easy if we hold our pace."

"Suppose they heard us at the rancho?" Encizo inquired.

"One problem at a time. We were expecting opposition, anyway. Let's play it as it comes."

"And Trask?"

The question came from Bolan's flank, one of the Mounties with a grim expression on his face.

"We don't have time for funerals. Conceal the body now, and we can come back for him later if we get the chance."

"That stinks."

"You bet it does. I'm open to suggestions if you feel a brainstorm coming on—but make it quick."

The Mountie glared at Bolan for a moment, then finally shook his head in a reluctant negative.

"Right, then," McPherson said. "Let's get him out of sight among those rocks. Don't leave the ammunition or grenades. We'll need them where we're going."

Bolan turned to face their guide, a bandage stark and white against his cheek. "You've done enough, Fernando. We can carry it from here."

The villager was ready with an argument, but he thought better of it. Maybe he was thinking of his wife at home, the little boy whom they'd nearly lost to violence days ago. So recently, but it had been a lifetime for the men who didn't walk away.

At last Fernando nodded, swallowing his pride in favor of survival. "Take the river as your guide," he said. "Four miles downstream it fills a lake. From there you travel on Costanza's land. The house lies north and west."

They shook hands solemnly, the Executioner aware of what it cost Fernando to retreat and leave them to their own devices. Stubborn pride was all some mountain peasants had to call their own, and backing off from any fight, regardless of the odds, would leave a scar.

Still, the devotion to his family was stronger than the man's private needs. Mack Bolan watched him go, then turned to face the other members of the team. "Four miles and then some. We're wasting time."

They fell into step behind him, their scuffling footsteps swallowed by the night.

15

Luis Costanza was sipping brandy, staring at the dark line of the mountains when his houseman brought him a report from the perimeter. Shots fired. Position difficult—if not impossible—to ascertain. There had been rifles, automatic weapons, but the noise had subsided prior to the acquisition of a fix. A spot-check of the forest outposts would be made without delay.

Costanza frowned but made no reply as he dismissed the messenger. Without specifics he couldn't evaluate the news or draw conclusions. Were they facing an assault, or had his troops decided it was time to liven up their vigil with some target practice in the dark?

Bad luck for any of the gunners who provoked a false alarm with reckless gunplay. He'd see the bastards skinned alive and staked on anthills if it came to that, a lesson to the others who believed that working night patrol was some elaborate game.

Yet Costanza felt his stomach churning as he scanned the distant tree line, wishing that his eyes could pierce the darkness and reveal his enemies.

Who would be brave enough—or fool enough—to risk a move against his home?

If the police were on their way, F-2 or the DAS, he would have been forewarned, and they wouldn't approach his rancho through the darkness overland in any case. Colombian authorities preferred to stage their grand, infrequent raids by air, employing helicopters thoughtfully provided by the President of the United States. They came complete with television crews and klieg lights, when they came at all. There would be no sneaking through the jungle like commandos with the risk of actually taking someone by surprise.

That left Costanza's unofficial enemies, and while the list of names was long enough to fill a midsize telephone directory, he could dismiss the bulk of them without a second thought. Small-timers, most of them, without the nerve or physical resources to attempt a raid. Of those who had the money, guns and men two names sprang instantly to mind.

Rodriguez and Mercado had been eager to accept Costanza's olive branch a few days earlier, along with his assurances that he wasn't responsible for the attacks on their homes and businesses. So far so good... But he'd promised them solutions and he still had none to give. Worse yet, both dealers had been hit by new assaults within the past two days.

Hostilities were renewed, and if they started looking for a villain, they might look no farther than Costanza's ranch before they organized a counterstroke.

One possibility remained. He'd also thrown the gauntlet down to unknown enemies with the abduction of Dominga Franco and her child. The aim had been exposure of his opposition, but the stalkers might have something else in mind.

Some vengeance of their own, perhaps.

So be it.

One way or another he'd know their faces and their names. If they were rash enough to face Costanza in his own backyard, so much the better. He had troops enough on hand to meet the threat, contain it and dispose of any evidence at leisure.

The more Costanza thought about it now, the more he liked the notion of a showdown at the rancho. It wasn't unlike a western movie, boasting all the classic elements of drama—heroes, villains, even damsels in distress.

This time, however, it would be Costanza's turn to write the script. He was the star and the director, deciding who would live and who would die. As for the leading lady, she had evidently served her purpose as a lure. Costanza saw no reason for her to survive beyond the final wrap.

He called the houseman back and issued orders for his troops on the perimeter. He wanted a determination on the source of gunfire, but the hunters would refrain from any further contact with the enemy unless their quarry tried to flee. If there was evidence of an advance on the rancho, they should stay well back and follow at a distance, waiting for instructions once the trap was sprung.

Costanza didn't know his enemies by name, but he could feel their need for contact, and he didn't mean to disappoint them. Soon now, if they knew enough to find their way, they'd have all the contact they could stand.

And more.

Costanza smiled, the first time in a week or more. He left his study, moving past the guards and feeling them behind him as he neared the basement stairs.

He had a melodrama to direct, and it was time the leading lady learned her part.

THE LAST LEG of their march was downhill all the way. They made fair time, with Bolan leading, ever conscious of the risk that trackers might be following. One of the snipers had been radio-equipped, but short of waiting at the site, they had no way of knowing whether he'd called for help before he died.

Encizo had the walkie-talkie now, and they'd covered nearly three-quarters of a mile when an excited voice came on the air, demanding an acknowledgment in Spanish. Encizo replied as best he could, delivering assurances that all was well and breaking off the link, but Bolan read dissatisfaction on his face.

"What gives?"

The Cuban shrugged. "It sounded like they bought it."

Bolan knew he was hedging, and he understood the reason why. Despite the radio's distortion, odd inflections or an unfamiliar voice could give the game away. There could be predetermined passwords whose omission told the caller he had a ringer on the line. And if the scouts decided they should double-check by dropping over for a face-to-face...

"You did your best," he said. "Let's move."

At every step the Executioner was ready for another burst of gunfire from the darkness, bullets whispering among them, smacking into flesh. As one who had experienced the loss of comrades under fire, he recognized McPherson's pain, the guilt and anger that prevented it from showing through. If the sergeant made it home again, it would be his job to report Trask's death, a life cut off too soon in the pursuit of unacknowledged goals.

The river led them onward, down a rocky slope turned almost gentle now with smooth stones underfoot. The canyon walls were tall and stark above them, blotting out a major portion of the sky. The warrior concentrated on the ground in front of him, selecting each step carefully, alert for traps as well as snipers in the trees.

How far?

Fernando's estimate of four miles to the flatland should be fairly accurate, but they'd have to wait and see. Beyond that point the probability of meeting a patrol was geometrically increased as they approached Costanza's home. With one firefight behind them, one man dead and two more slightly wounded, they could ill afford a string of random clashes going in.

And if the enemy was waiting for them when they made their move, what then?

The answer came as naturally to Bolan as the beating of his heart. They'd already come too far and paid too dearly for a scrub. Whatever happened at Costanza's ranch, they'd proceed and give it everything they had.

Defeat was always possible, but Bolan didn't know the meaning of surrender to an enemy. He'd press on while life remained, and if the bastards took him down, he wouldn't go alone.

How far?

The warrior smiled.

Not far enough for Bolan's enemies to hide.

DOMINGA FRANCO CEASED her pacing for a moment, listening to Andeana turn and whimper in her sleep. Bad dreams, she thought, and who could blame the child with all that she'd suffered in the past two days?

Her father's death, to start—a tragedy the childish mind could scarcely comprehend. It seemed to Andeana that her papá must be hiding, playing games, if only she could seek him out and bring him home again.

The ambush on their flight from Medellín was something else entirely. This time Andeana had been shaken by the sound of gunfire and explosions, terrified despite Dominga's efforts to protect her from the sight of bodies in the street, the stench of burning men.

How many adults could survive what she'd seen without some damage to the heart and soul?

They hadn't been molested since the battle on the highway, though a couple of Dominga's captors had regarded her with something close to hunger in their eyes. It was apparent the gunmen had their orders, and they dared not step across the line.

So far.

They'd been flown from Medellín by helicopter to a lavish ranch that Dominga recognized at once from prior descriptions in the press. Luis Costanza hadn't greeted them, but she'd almost felt him watching as the guards had conveyed them to their cell.

The prison was a basement room, but furnished with a sense of style. They had a bathroom, a double bed, a dresser and a closet to themselves. Dominga saw by her watch that two hours had passed before a servant brought them food on china plates that could almost be seen through if they were held to the light.

Dominga had no appetite, but Andeana ate her fill. In truth, the food had looked delicious—rare roast beef, potatoes and a crisp green salad on the side—but thinking of Sigfrido's death, her husband's recent murder and Costanza sitting safe upstairs combined to kill Dominga's appetite.

It must be dark by now, she thought, and the authorities would have a search in progress, scouring the province. They'd know enough to point a finger at Costanza certainly, but there would be no solid evidence. Dominga knew that much from listening to conversations where her husband had lamented the corruption in their government, the skill with which Costanza managed to conceal his tracks.

A problem had been nagging at Dominga's mind since the abduction, but she had it now. Her enemies hadn't disguised themselves, and there had been no blindfolds on the helicopter ride, no effort to conceal their destination from Dominga or her child. At first the combination of her fear and anger had been strong enough to overpower logic, but she understood the meaning of their reckless actions.

The gunmen hadn't bothered with precautions because they meant to leave no witnesses alive. Whatever plan Costanza had in mind, she realized that he didn't intend to set them free. When she and Andeana had served their purpose, playthings in Costanza's hands, they'd be killed.

Somehow the certain knowledge of her own impending death had failed to terrify Dominga Franco. Rather, it had stoked her inner rage as she foresaw the execution of her only child, the final vestige of her sweet life with Benito wiped away.

And yet, if all Costanza wanted was her death, the gunners could have saved some time and energy in Medellín when she was helpless and surrounded by at least a dozen guns. There must be *something* he desired that called for her cooperation—or at least her presence. Some negotiation . . . or an ultimatum to the government perhaps.

And if he needed her alive . . .

As if in answer to her thoughts, Dominga heard a sound of footsteps in the corridor outside. A key turned in the lock, and she was staring at the man who gave the order for her husband's death.

Costanza glanced at Andeana, almost smiling as he closed the door. When he addressed Dominga, he was careful not to raise his voice.

"The child sleeps well?"

"As well as possible, considering the past two days."

"Of course. I understand."

"You should."

She caught a momentary flicker in his eyes—not guilt, more like irritation—but Costanza hid it well.

"Your husband understood the risk he assumed in taking on his job."

"And that excuses murder?"

"There are always casualties in war," Costanza said, apparently believing it.

"What risks did *we* assume? My child and I have no part in your so-called war."

"Unfortunately that isn't the case. You're celebrities since... Well, let's say that circumstance has cast you in the public eye. Today the government in Bogotá professes deep concern at what becomes of you."

"A rich man like you, I wouldn't think you'd need the ransom."

"No." Costanza managed something like a smile. "I've asked no money in return for your release."

"What then?" Dominga couldn't block the question, even knowing that the prospect of relief was a sadistic sham.

"A bit of information," he replied. "Perhaps assistance in disposing of a certain problem that has come to light."

"Your army isn't large enough? You need the government to help you now?"

"With problems that the government created, yes. For all I know your husband might have been involved himself."

Dominga stood her ground. "Benito never spoke about his plans at home."

"A wise decision," Costanza said. "Never fear. I have no plans to question you . . . or her."

Behind Dominga Andeana stirred in bed but didn't wake. Dominga kept her voice pitched low as she replied. "You've made a serious mistake. My husband's murder broke all ties between myself and Bogotá."

"And yet you were escorted to the airport by the DAS."

"A simple courtesy. The man in charge—one of the men you butchered—was a family friend."

"You must have other friends, as well."

"None weak enough to deal with scum like you."

Costanza stiffened, angry color rising in his face, but he restrained himself. "You speak your mind," he said at last. "A trait some men would find offensive in a woman, but I disagree. If I were to suggest a change in your behavior, I'd ask you to select your words with someone else in mind." He glanced beyond her toward the bed where Andeana slept.

Dominga felt her blood run cold. "I must apologize."

"And denigrate your courage? Not at all. In future, though . . ." He left it hanging, turning toward the door.

Dominga hadn't planned on speaking, but the words burst from her in a rush. "How long before you make the trade?"

A stupid question, knowing there would be no trade. She was as good as dead.

Costanza shrugged. "A day or two perhaps if all goes well. The answer lies with those you call your friends. It might be necessary that we put the two of you on tape to prove you are still alive."

"As you require."

"In that case, pleasant dreams."

He closed the door behind him as he left, the lock engaging with a muffled snap.

A day or two perhaps. And when Costanza got the information—or the "help"—he wanted, they'd both be killed. Dominga knew it in her heart.

But she wouldn't go down without a fight.

She checked on Andeana again, making sure the child was still asleep, then started scouring the room for a potential weapon. There was nothing in the drawers that she could use, and the closet was empty, save for a half-dozen mothballs on the shelf.

She had a sudden revelation, startled by the plan's simplicity—the bathroom. It was perfect.

Turning on the light, she softly closed the bathroom door, protecting Andeana from the noise, and went to work.

THE HELICOPTERS SAT like giant prehistoric insects in the middle of a parking lot, surrounded by a score of men carrying automatic weapons. The hulking outline of a warehouse shielded them from passersby who might have stopped and stared. Twin floodlights bleached expectant faces as Rodriguez and Mercado crossed the asphalt.

Mercado still had nagging doubts about the plan, but he'd failed to conjure up alternatives. He still had time to pull his soldiers out, but then Rodriguez would become his enemy, as well. And if truth were told, Mercado had a not-so-secret itch to see Costanza broken, stripped of all the power he'd managed to accumulate while others struggled to survive.

José Mercado wasn't struggling exactly, but he could have been a great deal richer. And he would be soon when they'd finally dispatched one greedy pig to his final reward.

Revenge was sweet, but profit made it all the better to enjoy.

The difficulty would be coming out of it alive. Compared to the defenses at Costanza's rancho, twenty men had little hope of pulling off a major coup. With that in mind, another thirty would be traveling by jeep and truck to keep Costanza's sentries busy while the helicopters made their strike.

Mercado would ideally have preferred to stay at home and wait for film clips on the television news, but with Rodriguez heading up the strike force, he couldn't afford to seem less macho. Nor, on second thought, could he afford to have *his* soldiers taking orders from Rodriguez in the field. Surrendering authority would set a lethal precedent that might return to haunt him someday.

He spent a moment with his crew chief while Rodriguez did the same. Their men were evenly divided, but Mercado would be riding with Rodriguez in the lead ship while his second-in-command took charge of the directions for the second wave. It seemed a needless risk, both leaders jammed together in a single aircraft, but Rodriguez had convinced him that a show of "solidarity" was paramount.

Their plan, at least, was pure simplicity. While ground troops struck at the perimeter and drew Costanza's gunmen from the house, the airborne team would slip in at their backs and raze the mansion, making sure Costanza was among the casualties. As for the woman and her child... Well, they would have to take their chances with the rest.

Mercado's crew chief had an AK-47 waiting for him, as well as extra magazines. He hesitated, balancing the automatic rifle in his hands until he saw Rodriguez brandishing an M-16.

No point in taking chances, after all.

Mercado trusted Raul Rodriguez to a point—as much as he'd ever trusted anyone—but growing up an orphan on the streets and trafficking in cocaine had convinced him that anyone was capable of treachery at any time. Today his interests coincided with Rodriguez's in eliminating the Costanza empire, but division of the spoils would place new strain on their relationship. If Raul decided he was better off without a partner, seizing on the chaos of a firefight as the cover for a calculated act, Mercado would be ready for him.

Waiting.

Rodriguez beckoned, and Mercado joined him at the other helicopter, watching as the gunmen climbed aboard. The pilots were already firing up their engines, rotors turning slowly overhead, the backwash ruffling Mercado's hair. He hated that—a fortune spent on barbers to achieve a certain style—but it couldn't be helped.

On board he took a seat and cinched the safety harness across his chest. The act of flying didn't frighten him, but he preferred wide-body jets with bulk enough to guarantee that midair turbulence would rarely cause a ripple in his drink. The helicopter smelled of fuel and motor oil, the engines loud enough that he was forced to shout when he tried to talk with Rodriguez.

They were flying into combat in a ship that sounded as if it was about to fall apart.

Mercado closed his eyes on lift-off, then opened them again when they were safely airborne. He consoled himself with a statistic—drawn from sources he couldn't recall—that said most aircraft crashed on takeoff, or on landing. Relatively few experienced a failure while in flight and plunged to earth.

Unless, of course, someone was shooting at them.

As Costanza's men would be, the moment they approached his grand estate.

Mercado closed his mind to images of smoking, twisted steel and melted rotor blades. A worrier by nature, he was facing risk enough from his acknowledged enemy without anticipating acts of God.

They started north, and Mercado glanced down at the city before it slipped away. Beneath his feet the lights seemed small and far away, like rippling coals of fire.

IT WAS APPROACHING midnight when they reached the flats, with scattered trees and grassland stretching out in front of them. They took five on a rocky hillside, Bolan checking out his compass readings, verifying the direction to Costanza's spread.

They'd been walking on the dealer's land for close to half an hour, though there had been no warning signs or fences. Everyone in Antioquia Province knew Costanza and the boundaries of his vast estate, and most of them had sense enough to stay away. Free access was by invitation only, and the penalties for trespassing were harsh indeed.

Two miles remained before they reached their destination. The men were tired from the climb, the march on rugged ground and their battle with the snipers. Two miles would mean another hour if they met no opposition on the way, and after that it would be each man for himself within the fragile outline of their strategy.

"It's time."

No sooner had he spoken than the Executioner saw headlights in the distance, rapidly approaching on a hard collision course. He blinked and watched them double, blinked again and saw no change.

A pair of vehicles, most likely four-wheel drive, had been dispatched to scout the river and surrounding landscape for intruders. Did it mean they were blown, or were they looking at a regular patrol?

No way to answer that as Bolan put his troops in motion, scattering for cover on the rocky ground. The men with silenced weapons formed the first defensive line, the Executioner among them, the sleek Beretta 93-R in his hand.

He recognized the sound of jeeps a hundred yards out, the vehicles maintaining course and closing on the canyon's mouth as if a beacon had been lit to summon them. He wondered once again about the snipers, and the query Encizo had tried to answer on the liberated radio.

He watched the jeeps diverge, one veering off in each direction, rolling toward the tree line and the rugged hills beyond. It would take more than four-wheel drive to climb those slopes, but they could scout along the edges.... It seemed that was exactly what they had in mind. A hundred yards to either side of his position, Bolan saw the jeeps turn back, converging in a manner that would bring them back together roughly twenty feet from where he lay.

The drivers took their time on this part of the detail, fairly creeping as the shotgun riders played their spotlights over trees and tangled undergrowth. Each jeep was fitted with a .50-caliber machine gun on the deck, the triggermen alert and spoiling for a fight.

Exposure or coincidence?

He didn't know and didn't really care.

They had a golden opportunity in front of them if they could make it work, and Bolan meant to try. He whispered curt instructions to Encizo and heard the Cuban pass them on.

It would be tricky, but they were bound to make the effort. If they pulled it off, it meant a fresh start on the trail and a chance to fox their enemies.

He watched and waited while the jeeps drew nearer, slowing almost to a halt before they met downrange. The spotlights made another sweep, and Bolan prayed that all his men were safely undercover as the probing beams swept by. He half expected an explosion from the .50s, but the night was quiet, muffled voices wafting to him on the breeze.

He chose the gunner on the right, the 93-R set for 3-round bursts as Bolan sighted down the slide. He took a breath and held it, using both hands on the grip. Then he squeezed the trigger, tracking on in search of other targets instantly, not waiting to assess the damage from his fire.

He had a fleeting, fragmentary image of the gunner pitching backward, dead hands giving up the machine gun as he fell. Around him other weapons stuttered through the tubes of their suppressors, picking off the second gunner, targeting the drivers and their shotgun riders in a cloud-burst of precision fire. The warrior had his sights fixed on another silhouette when it lurched sideways, twitching with the impact of a parabellum burst, and then went limp.

All done.

They rushed the idling jeeps and dragged the bodies clear, concealing them among the rocks. Katz slid behind the wheel of one vehicle, his comrades scrambling in around him, with Encizo on the gun. The Mounties had their seats staked out in number two as Bolan took the wheel.

Two miles.

Make that ten minutes if they took their time on unfamiliar ground.

Before he put the jeep into gear, Bolan nodded to McCarter and saw the Briton pick up his radio and flash the signal that would put Grimaldi in the air.

All systems go.

Costanza had a shock in store for him, and Bolan couldn't wait to see the dealer's face.

16

The silenced pistol Yakov Katzenelenbogen carried was a Browning double-action that used custom-made subsonic loads. The fat suppressor threaded to the weapon's muzzle helped reduce its recoil, but it also made the piece feel over-long and clumsy in his good hand.

Still, inconvenience hardly mattered at the moment, or the range he'd be shooting from.

The jeeps were drawing closer to Costanza's hardsite—close enough, in fact, that Katz could see the lighted windows of the great house, shining like a beacon in the night. The photographs acquired by aerial reconnaissance informed him that the dark mass on their left would be the zoo, a first impression soon confirmed by feline cries that would have sounded more at home in Africa.

Katz had the Browning ready in his left hand, stainless-steel prosthesis managing the wheel as they approached a checkpoint fifty yards ahead. The Israeli checked his rearview mirror, making sure Bolan was in place four lengths behind. "One sound and everybody knows we've crashed the party, right?"

"I heard that," James replied.

"Make sure it's *all* you hear."

"I'm set," the former SEAL assured him, thumbing back the hammer on a silencer-equipped Beretta as he spoke.

"Okay."

The headlights helped, but in another moment they were close enough for both young sentries to decide there was something wrong—too many bodies in the jeep, for one thing; unfamiliar faces as grim as death.

Katz shot the gunner on his side, a double punch that opened blowholes in his chest and pitched him backward, sprawling on the grass. His weapon spun away and landed out of reach beyond his twitching fingertips.

A sound reminding Katz of a muffled sneeze came from James's side, and the second gunner melted out of sight. The Chicago badass flashed the thumbs-up signal, Katz repeating it for Bolan's benefit in case the Executioner had any doubts.

The jeep rolled on.

Katz kept the pistol in his lap with the safety off. He might need it again before they reached the house.

From that point on he knew that silence wouldn't matter in the least.

GRIMALDI NOSED the Cobra gunship north, the Río Nechi serving as his guide. Experience had taught him how to deal with combat nerves, but coping didn't mean the nerves weren't there.

It only meant you didn't let them show.

The call from Bolan's team was more or less on time. A miracle, all things considered, and Grimaldi didn't let it bother him that there had been no word on their success so far. They'd acquired some wheels, and they were going in— which should have meant everything was jake.

It *should* have, right.

But Grimaldi had worked with Bolan long enough and close enough to know the guy would try to carry out his mission in the face of overwhelming odds regardless of his personal condition or the likelihood of going down in flames. It had to seem like Christmas, with a crack squad on his heels. No way the Executioner would scrub it now with hostages involved.

At least they hadn't lost the radio.

They'd waltzed around the dealer long enough in Grimaldi's opinion, setting up the stage to take him down. If they'd iced the bastard earlier, Benito Franco might still be alive, his wife and daughter safe at home.

The pilot caught himself before the "what if" game got out of hand. A man could lose his grip on sanity, considering the errors he'd made, the consequences that arose from each mistake.

Costanza was a predator, and Franco had been working overtime to bring him down before the Phoenix team had sat down to plot their strategy at Stony Man Farm. Considering the dealer's record, taking Franco out had been a natural response, a strategy that had been used to good effect on previous occasions—killing judges, cabinet ministers, police. As for the snatch that followed . . . Well, if there was guilt enough to go around, Grimaldi was prepared to take his share.

But first it was Costanza's turn.

Rodriguez and Mercado would be postscripts if the team had the time and opportunity, but both of them were hurting as it was. If one or both slipped through the net, the DAS could try to make a case while they were scrambling to claim the scattered pieces from Costanza's fall.

Assuming the bastard fell.

Grimaldi knew the risks inherent in presumption when your life was riding on the line. The one sure thing about a combat situation was that there *were* no sure things. That rule applied, in spades, when you were going in outnumbered and outgunned on unfamiliar ground.

But they were going in with air support, damn right.

The cavalry was on its way.

Grimaldi might not turn the tide, but he'd kick some ass and wake Costanza up to the reality that nothing came without a price attached. If there was any chance at all, Grimaldi meant to grab it by the throat and wring it dry. If they were looking at a surefire loser, he could still go out in style.

He pushed the gloomy thoughts aside and focused on his destination, mentally subtracting the miles and reckoning that he was nearly halfway there. Another fifteen minutes, twenty tops, and he'd have his shot at bringing down Costanza's house.

It was a prospect Grimaldi had been looking forward to for the past nine days.

If only Bolan and the rest were still around when he arrived.

The pilot didn't count himself as a religious man, but he remembered how to pray. Some things, once learned, are never quite forgotten.

Anyway, he told himself, it couldn't hurt.

This time around the good guys needed all the help they could get.

THE BASIC PLAN HAD altered only slightly when they found their wheels. Instead of creeping past the outer guards as best they could, the Phoenix team would bluff and kill their way past checkpoints leading onto the estate, and once onsite their ultimate objectives would remain the same.

For Bolan and the RCMP officers the target was Costanza's mansion, leaving Katz and company to cope with yardmen, sweep the servants' quarters and create whatever havoc they could raise by throwing open pens and cages in the dealer's private zoo. With the diverse approach, he thought they stood a decent chance of heading off Costanza when he tried to cut and run.

But, even so, it was risky.

A cautious estimate would show his team outnumbered five or six to one, and Bolan knew the hard stats might be double that. Costanza had prepared himself for war, and that meant soldiers on alert around the house and grounds with other teams on call from the perimeter. They might be looking at a hundred guns or more, instead of forty-five or fifty. They had to forge ahead regardless of the odds.

Retreat not only ran against the grain, but it would be suicide at this late stage of the proceedings. They'd passed the point of no return when they snatched the jeeps and took out the first two sentries.

But so far they were still alive, and Jack was on the way— winged fury, and an equalizer the Costanza troops wouldn't be counting on.

If only he wasn't too late.

The second checkpoint blew their small advantage of surprise. One of the lookouts had a sharper eye than his companions, counting heads in time to shout a warning. He even managed to release a burst of automatic rifle fire, but it was high and to the left. The .50-caliber machine gun on Katz's jeep cut loose in answer, ripping through Costanza's gunmen like so many scarecrows, and the way was clear.

For all of forty seconds.

There was no alarm, per se, but none was necessary with a burst of automatic gunfire unleashed within two hundred yards of the mansion. Strategic floodlights blazed to life around the house and captured gunners on the run, converging singly and in groups on the scene of the disturbance.

Bolan killed his headlights just as Katz did the same. They parted company on cue, one jeep proceeding toward the servants' quarters and the zoo enclosures, while the other made a loop around the east side of the house. At Bolan's back a Mountie named Moore had the .50 primed and ready, holding back until they started drawing fire or had a target worth his time.

The first two gunners opened fire at forty yards, or thereabouts, their submachine guns filling the air with 5.56 mm hornets. Moore answered with a burst that chopped up divots in the grass around them, dropping them together in a heap.

Not bad.

The Executioner was driving with a CAR-15 across his lap, the safety off, but he left all the firing to McPherson's raiders as they made their run around the house. Expensive wheels were parked beneath a carport, and a long burst from the .50-caliber machine gun turned them into ventilated scrap. When gunners darted into view and angry muzzle-flashes lit the darkness on their right, the big machine gun and a pair of automatic rifles rolled them up and canceled out the threat.

"The floodlights!" Bolan shouted, and Moore brought his weapon around, the hot brass scattering in all directions, one shell bouncing off the steering wheel to drop at Bolan's feet. It took a moment, but he got results, the west wing of the mansion going dark except for lights that burned inside.

"Hang on!"

He hit the brakes and killed the engine, bailing out a heartbeat later with McPherson on his heels. Behind them Corporal Benning was bringing up the rear, Moore staying with the jeep to cover their advance. A stream of armor-piercing rounds tracked right to left across the upstairs windows, putting out a couple of the inside lights before it dipped to sweep across the broad expanse of lawn. More gunners were caught without a place to hide, their bodies twisting and jerking as they fell.

A pair of sentries had the porch secured when Bolan got there, swiveling to greet him as a burst of 5.56 mm tumblers cut their legs from under them. They fell across his line of fire, McPherson joining in the carnage with a short burst of his own.

In the excitement no one had considered taking time to lock the door. Costanza's house was covered by the best troops Medellín could offer, armed and trained to fight by Isaac Auerbach and company. There should have been no way for hostile gunners to set foot inside.

But in they were, and it was party time.

LUIS COSTANZA NEARLY missed the outbreak of the battle, muffled as the gunfire was by distance and the sturdy walls around him. Still, his ears picked up the faint jackhammer sound of a machine gun, lighter weapons chiming in a moment later, and he knew the raid was on.

He should have been dismayed, but there was only mild surprise that his assailants had survived this long. Costanza had expected the perimeter patrols to head them off before they came within a mile of his retreat, but something obviously had gone wrong.

The evening's great surprise was that Costanza didn't care.

In fact, he felt a sort of strange exhilaration at the prospect of confronting those who'd conspired to bring his empire down. It was poetic justice that he should be present for the kill.

With any luck he might be privileged enough to finish off one or two of them himself.

Despite the early rumors out of Medellín, Costanza put no faith in the ridiculous assertion that a single man had been responsible for his misfortune in the past few days. It was impossible, a judgment readily confirmed by officers who visited the scene of carnage where the People's Army of Colombia had been massacred. Ballistics indicated several different weapons used against the rebels, fired from angles and positions that precluded one man doing all the work. A team of four or five was probable, and he was betting on a larger number—possibly a dozen, based on the damage they'd caused so far.

However many there might be, they were about to die. Costanza smiled, deciding he'd save a few choice cuts when it was over, just to feed the great cats in his zoo.

But first the kill.

He found a pair of riflemen on-station when he left his study, dark eyes flicking from Costanza to the stairs and back again. The gunners were on edge, prepared to join the fighting if he ordered it, perhaps considering how long they had before the battle came to them.

"With me," he snapped, and they fell into step behind him, following along the corridor. Costanza ducked inside his game room and emerged a moment later with a shiny AK-47 in his hands. The bandolier of extra magazines across his chest was heavy, and perhaps unnecessary for a clash he expected to be brief at best. But he enjoyed the feeling and the way it made him look—a fighting leader, unafraid to lead his troops by bold example, worthy of respect.

If his display of raw machismo cheered the bodyguards, they managed to conceal it well. Costanza missed the warning glance that passed between them, something in the eyes that spoke of doubt...perhaps a trace of fear. It passed, and neither one of them considered balking as Costanza started for the stairs.

There might be danger outside, but they were dealing with a man they knew would execute them both without a second thought. At least outside they had a chance.

They were almost at the stairs before Costanza heard the front door open, crashing heavily against the wall as someone—several someones—forced their way inside. He froze and flicked the safety off his AK-47, listening. The enemy had breached his very home. A change of plan was indicated, and he spun to face his bodyguards. "You two," he snapped. "Downstairs!"

CALVIN JAMES HIT the ground running, ducking a wild burst from the .50 and sprinting all-out as he left the jeep behind him, breaking for the noisy darkness of the zoo.

The animals were going crazy, the gunfire stoking fears engendered by the tremors that had kept them pacing restlessly since dusk. James heard the big cats snarling in their pits and cages, monkeys screeching as they hurled themselves around their pens. The zebras and the antelopes were mute, but panic kept them moving, ripples in the herd that shifted back and forth across a fenced enclosure.

He started with the monkeys, working up to larger game, bolt cutters snipping open padlocks, playing havoc with the strands of chain-link fence. James didn't wait around to watch the prison break, already moving toward the zebras and their running mates before the first sly gibbon made his move. It wouldn't take them long once they got started, and they didn't need a one-man cheering section in the wings.

It struck him that the zebras might run back and forth inside their pen all night despite an open gate, so he took down a whole section of the fence. It wasn't hard—more time-consuming than exhausting—but it nearly got him killed.

The zoo was low-priority in terms of armed defense, especially with Costanza's palace coming under fire, and James was startled when a sentry blundered toward him in the darkness, questioning his sanity in Spanish that was angry and obscene. A silent parabellum round resolved the controversy, and he spent another moment scouting high and low for other guards before returning to his task.

Costanza's bears were sluggish off the mark, which suited Calvin fine. He spent no extra time outside their pens once he'd clipped the locks and jammed the gates with stones to hold them wide.

The reptiles were a problem. Dumping out the snakes was no big deal, although it called for fancy footwork with the cobras and revived unpleasant memories of his encounter on the trail. The crocodiles, by contrast, stubbornly refused to leave their pool, but Calvin dropped a ten-foot length of fence and wished them well.

He saved the cats for last, deliberately, deciding it was better if he finished off the bulk of his assignment first before a Bengal tiger accidentally mistook him for a midnight snack. The animals were visibly excited, snarling at him as he severed padlocks on the gates that held them prisoner. It was an awkward trick, but Calvin managed to negotiate the clippers with the automatic pistol in his hand, his M-16 slung muzzle-down across his chest.

Instead of rushing at the open gate, the tigers circled warily, examining the stranger and his tools. Downrange, a couple of the lions were emerging from their pen, and James knew it was time to leave before someone invited him to stay for lunch.

Don't run, he told himself. They follow when you run. It makes them think you're afraid.

He holstered the Beretta, gripped the M-16 and started walking, keeping one eye on the open cages as he went.

He was almost out of sight before another tremor brought the tigers out in search of prey.

17

The weapon seemed ridiculous compared to Costanza's guns, but it was all she could find inside the Spartan rooms. Dominga had removed the float arm from the toilet tank, a ten-inch metal rod that she'd easily concealed inside the left sleeve of her blouse, one end secured beneath her watchband.

Ready.

It didn't possess sufficient weight to be a bludgeon, and the threaded ends were far from sharp, but it would serve her purpose if she had a chance to reach Costanza's face.

At one point in her life Dominga Franco had been a nurse in Bogotá. She knew the human body inside out, but it had never crossed her mind before this night that she'd have to use her knowledge as a weapon, seeking to obliterate a life instead of saving one.

The difference, obviously, was her child.

Dominga had no reason to believe she could rescue Andeana from the fate Costanza had in mind for both of them, but she could make him pay.

She'd been watching Andeana sleep when gunfire suddenly erupted on the grounds outside—machine guns, interspersed with what she took for rifle fire and pistol shots. The sounds were drawing closer when her daughter stirred, sat up in bed and suddenly began to cry.

Dominga knelt beside her, wrapping the girl in her arms, the metal rod inside her sleeve forgotten for the moment.

She was thinking past the gunfire, trying to decipher what it meant to her, the future of her child.

A raid? Perhaps the DAS?

She knew Sigfrido had loyal friends in the department who'd risk their lives to avenge his death. The problem would have been persuading officers of any rank to authorize a raid against Costanza's home when there was no substantial evidence to justify a search.

Or was there?

Had Costanza failed to cover his tracks somehow? She knew a number of his gunmen had been shot when she and Andeana were abducted. Could it be that one of them had talked when in custody or carried evidence on his person that would lead the DAS back to the dealer?

There was one more possibility that came to mind, perhaps more plausible, but it did nothing to relieve her mind. Dominga knew her captor was a man with enemies throughout the underworld, and it was possible that some of them were in the act of trying to assassinate Costanza. First inclined to wish them luck, Dominga shortly realized that victory by any of Costanza's rivals, here and now, would have no positive effect upon her own condition. As a witness, she'd be expendable—worse yet, a liability—and killing her, together with her child, would be a simple act of cleaning house.

There were no windows in the basement cell, and sounds were muffled by the walls and ceiling, but she felt the shock of an explosion somewhere overhead. Grenades? A bomb?

What if they set the house on fire and drove Costanza out? Would she and Andeana be forgotten? Left to burn alive?

If it came down to that, Dominga knew her duty. Andeana's suffering the past two days had been enough without a fiery death to cap the grim experience. If there was fire, Dominga would be forced to intervene for mercy's sake.

And, time permitting, she'd also find a way to spare herself.

For now it was enough to hold her daughter, listening to automatic weapons, waiting for the telltale smell of smoke. She almost missed the sound of footsteps, drawing closer to her door, before a key turned in the lock.

Costanza stood before her, looking like a mountain bandit with a bandolier across his chest and an automatic rifle in his hands.

He stepped inside the room and raised his weapon, covering the two of them as if he feared they were about to break and run. In fact, it crossed Dominga's mind, but it was tantamount to suicide without a plan.

"It's time for us to go," Costanza told her, his twisted smile seeming out of place. "You, first."

THE FOYER of Costanza's house was larger than the barracks Bolan once had occupied with thirteen other grunts in Vietnam. Above his head a massive gold-and-crystal chandelier played fractured beams of light across the ceiling, offering the impression of a huge kaleidoscope. Connecting doors on Bolan's left stood open on a lavish sitting room. The tall doors on his right were closed. In front of them the spiral staircase seemed specifically designed for making entrances and greeting guests in style.

Except that the two hardguys rushing downstairs at the moment had submachine guns in their hands. Both of them were hyped, and they began to fire as soon as they made target acquisition, spraying bullets high and wide without a real attempt to aim.

It was a fair enough approach for panic situations, but the gunners were a bit too hasty coming down. One of them lost his footing and stumbled on the stairs. Bullets from his Uzi started chipping crystal from the chandelier before he caught the banister. Behind him, stopping short to ward off a collision, his surprised companion made a perfect target for perhaps a second and a half.

It was all the time Bolan needed. He fired from the hip, 5.56 mm tumblers ripping flesh and woodwork as they raked his adversary from groin to chin. The impact dropped the guy onto the stairs and gravity took over, prompting the collision that the gunner spent his final heartbeats trying to avoid.

The lead man lost his balance and his Uzi simultaneously, throwing out both hands to catch himself. It must have been a grim two seconds, knowing he was dead and that there was nothing he could do about it, but McPherson's weapon cut the moment short and squelched the gunner's cry of panic as he fell.

Two down, and Bolan knew it couldn't be that easy. No damn way at all. He crossed the foyer in a rush to check the sitting room and found it empty. Another door stood open on the far side of the room, darkness showing on the other side, but Bolan let it go. Costanza's mansion could become a hopeless maze if they began to run around the rooms and corridors pell-mell without a vestige of strategy.

Returning to the foyer, he was pleased to find Moore with the others, cradling an M-16 complete with 40 mm and M-203 launcher mounted underneath the barrel. He seemed unscathed, and Bolan wondered briefly whether he'd run the .50 dry, or merely tired of shooting sitting ducks.

"We haven't got much time," the Executioner reminded them. "The hostages could be in any one of eighty-odd rooms, and we don't know how many gunners are inside the house."

"Split up?" McPherson prompted.

"It's the only way we've got a shot."

"I'd favor two-man teams."

"Agreed. Your choice."

McPherson shrugged. "Benning, come with me. Moore, watch your ass."

"My specialty," the man answered, grinning.

Before they had a chance to separate, a violent tremor rocked the house and set the damaged chandelier to swinging overhead. Another shock came close behind the first, and Bolan heard the sound of breaking glassware in the sitting room.

"Bad timing," McPherson said.

"Maybe not," the Executioner replied. "A nice diversion couldn't hurt right now."

"Unless it brings the roof down on our heads."

"Think positive. You begin upstairs, and we'll check this floor."

"Suits me."

McPherson and Benning hit the stairs, with Bolan and Moore making for the closed doors on their right. No sooner had they cleared the foyer than the crystal chandelier broke free and plummeted to the floor, exploding into fragments on the marble floor.

A nice diversion, right.

Unless it brings the roof down on our heads.

Dismissing the potential risk, he rushed the tall oak doors and threw them open, entering a game room with Moore on his heels.

Four men for eighty-odd rooms, with no hard evidence the hostages were here . . . or even still alive.

GRIMALDI HAD a bird's-eye view of the eruption, homing on his target with the night spread out below him, deep and dark. Immune to tremors in the earth, his Cobra felt the shock waves of the blast transmitted through the air, and he controlled the gunship with an effort, altering his course to miss the worst of the debris that would be raining down in seconds flat.

He'd observed volcanic action in the past, but this was different. He watched the pyroclastic flow of lava eating up the countryside, advancing on Costanza's hardsite and the ground team he'd come to save.

Trees flamed on contact with the superheated wall of magma, sputtering like matches for an instant, swallowed up and gone the next. Where ferns and grasses took the place of trees, a firestorm raced before the lava flow, igniting vines and creepers, brightening the landscape with a hellish glow. Grimaldi almost felt that he could reach outside and warm his hands, but as it was, he concentrated on his goal and kept both hands on the controls.

Five minutes later he spotted Costanza's compound, a bright oasis in the night, the lava surging forward like a living thing, intent on merging one light with another. Opening the throttle, he outran the creeping fire and came in from the south, already seeking targets at a hundred yards.

Three sides of the Costanza mansion were illuminated by strategically positioned floodlights, tiny figures darting back and forth like roaches in a kitchen, startled by the glare. The eastern wing was dark, the lights extinguished somehow. Grimaldi left that side alone, suspecting Bolan and his troops had staged the blackout for their own convenience.

He finished one quick circuit of the property, already drawing scattered fire, and nosed the Cobra down into a strafing run. At fifty yards the 20 mm Gatling guns laid down a carpet of destruction, sentries jerking underneath the floods like puppets, sprawling lifeless on the grass.

One pass completed, he brought the Cobra back around, intensely conscious of the fact that part of Bolan's team was scheduled for attacks outside the house. They might be anywhere, a flitting shadow near the servants' quarters or a twisted body lying near the zoo. It made Grimaldi's job that much more difficult, but there were ways . . .

A speck of light on the periphery of vision, drawing closer by the moment, suddenly distracted him. He glanced around and recognized the running lights of two more choppers, closing from the south.

"Goddamn it!"

He'd have to check them out at once, determine whether they were government or private, and respond accordingly. If they were DAS, F-2 or military ships, the game was up. But, on the other hand, if they weren't official, then Grimaldi had a target he could live with. Two of them, in fact.

He took the Cobra up and out of there in search of altitude, a vantage point for scrutinizing his potential enemies and striking from their blind side if a strike was indicated.

Any moment now.

"Hang on," he whispered to himself. "Let's do it right."

COSTANZA KEPT the woman and her child in front of him, both covered with the AK-47 as they moved along the basement corridor. They hesitated at the stairs, but he instructed them to keep on going toward a metal door that formed a dead end for the empty hall.

In fact, the door was only a beginning, his escape hatch from the house, which had become a death trap.

He wasn't a coward, but Costanza saw no profit in a one-man showdown with his enemies when mercenary troops were trained and paid to deal with such emergencies. The safety of his hostages was paramount in order to guarantee Costanza's ultimate success, and he was wise enough to keep them from the line of fire.

Beyond the metal door a tunnel ran for close to ninety yards beneath the carport and the tennis courts, emerging in a shed beside Costanza's private heliport. The subterranean escape route was a modest form of life insurance for a man in his position, and the very fact of its existence was a secret from his rank-and-file subordinates. No more than a half-dozen members of Costanza's staff had seen the tunnel, and the four who had survived the past ten days were all aboveground, fighting for their lives.

His pilots would be warming up the helicopter by now. The two men had separate quarters near the helipad, and terms of their employment called for one to stay within a thirty-second run of the aircraft whenever it was on the ground. If there was any sign of an attack on the estate, they were under standing orders to prepare for takeoff, standing fast regardless of the danger to themselves until Costanza reached the helipad.

It never crossed the dealer's mind that he'd be deserted by his pilots in a crunch. They knew the penalty for failure, much less for betrayal of the man who signed their checks, and held their lives like fragile eggshells in his hands. The public fate of underlings who had committed lesser indiscretions strengthened their resolve, and there was no place in the world where they could hide from the cartel if they betrayed Costanza's trust.

He used a special key—its only copy locked inside a hidden safe upstairs—and swung the heavy door aside. His fingers found a wall switch, flicked it, and a row of naked bulbs lit up the tunnel.

"Go on," he ordered, waggling the muzzle of his weapon when the woman hesitated, clinging to her child.

"In there?"

It was a foolish question, but Costanza understood her fear. Unfortunately for Dominga Franco, understanding brought no sympathy.

"Move!" he snapped, the rifle thrusting forward in a gesture she could scarcely misinterpret.

They moved, Costanza bringing up the rear and pausing long enough to lock the metal door behind him. There was no point giving up trade secrets, even in the last extremity.

Traversing the escape route felt like being swallowed up alive. Costanza wasn't claustrophobic, but he never walked the tunnel's length without reflecting on the childhood myth of Jonah and the whale. He couldn't see the stairs that led to the surface, still too far away, but knowledge of their presence helped reduce the clammy feeling of his skin.

This whale would save his life by swallowing Costanza and his hostages. A few more moments would see him inside the prefab storage building, with the helicopter warming up outside.

And they'd all be safe.

Another shock wave rocked the ground, and he ignored the cracks that spiderwebbed the concrete walls and floor around him, etching patterns on the roof above his head.

Costanza doggedly refused to contemplate the danger of a cave-in, being trapped below ground, with his whereabouts unknown.

Impossible.

They'd be airborne soon, and he could watch the battle from a vantage point on high, observing every detail as his mercenaries turned the tide.

His victory was preordained.

The superrich and superpowerful were simply not allowed to lose.

18

Bolan and Moore met the gunners coming through a swinging door from what appeared to be the kitchen. The first man out stopped abruptly and jerked the trigger of his Ingram MAC-10 submachine gun. If he'd thought about it, he would probably have raised the weapon first instead of blowing off his own left foot.

The wounded shooter toppled backward with a cry of pain, colliding with the man behind him, triggering another burst before they both went down and blocked the kitchen doorway. The blast from the Ingram was a little closer, but it still missed Bolan by an easy yard, and he was firing back before his adversaries could recover from their shock.

Moore's M-16 and Bolan's CAR-15 were different models of the same piece used extensively in Vietnam, their carbon-copy chatter mingling as they raked the open doorway. The tangled, prostrate gunners were the first to die, another pair behind them soaking up their share of 5.56 mm tumblers, dropping in their tracks as two or three more backup shooters dived for cover.

A moment later Costanza's people started firing back, albeit blindly, poking guns around the corner at arm's length and spraying aimless rounds across the dining room. It was a poor technique for scoring hits, but they could hold the door all night unless...

The Executioner was reaching for a frag grenade when his companion flashed a grin and said, "Let me."

Moore braced the M-16 against his hip and fired the launcher mounted underneath its barrel, ducking under cover of the heavy dining table as the HE round went home. It struck the left side of the doorjamb, detonating with a flash of smoky thunder. A man-size portion of the wall collapsed.

The gunner buried underneath it never felt the weight.

His comrade had a sudden urge to live, retreating under cover of an aimless burst that whispered several feet above their heads. It was an easy shot, returning fire, and Bolan dropped him with a single round at thirty feet.

For all the trouble they'd taken getting there, the kitchen was a disappointment. Pots and pans and utensils were scattered everywhere by the tremors and the detonation of Moore's HE round. There was no further opposition from Costanza's troops.

Another door led Bolan and his companion through a pantry, circling back the way they'd come. New rooms were all empty, and the Executioner experienced brief empathy for laboratory rats inside a maze.

"We're getting nowhere," he declared. "Let's finish up along this corridor and try to find McPherson."

"Fine by me," Moore said.

They still had a half-dozen rooms to check before they cleared the hall, but Bolan knew they'd be empty. Most—or all—of the remaining troops were fighting on the grounds; Costanza might be with them, but the odds told Bolan that his quarry had eluded him.

How many exits from a house this size? Too many.

But if Costanza ran, and most especially if he took his captives with him, hiding on the grounds wouldn't be good enough. He needed *out,* and that meant wheels or wings.

"Come on!"

Another violent tremor shook the house, this one continuing for several moments, raining plaster dust on Bolan's head. Behind them, at the far end of the corridor, a window shattered, and the sound of a horrific blast cut through the other sounds of battle.

Moore braced himself against a buckled wall, the color draining from his face. "Sweet Jesus! Did Costanza have an ammo dump out there, or what?"

Half certain he knew the answer, Bolan doubled back to reach the shattered window, peering out across a battlefield at mountains in the middle distance.

One of them was on fire and spitting molten lava into the air. Bright, viscous streamers flowed down the mountainside and spread outward from its base, devouring the landscape like a fluid juggernaut, approaching yard by yard on a collision course with the Costanza hardsite.

"Not an ammo dump," he replied as the Mountie stepped to his side.

"We're fucked."

"Not yet."

Above the sounds of battle and the rumbling of the earth, the warrior's ears picked up another sound, familiar, offering at least a prospect of relief—a helicopter, swooping low and firing at the enemy.

"We're not fucked yet," he said. "We've still got wings."

But first, before they flew, he had to find Costanza and the hostages, or satisfy himself that they'd slipped the net. In either case it meant a critical delay, but it couldn't be helped.

If necessary, he'd have to stand and face the cleansing fire.

JOSÉ MERCADO CROSSED himself and gaped at the surging lava, both captivated by its beauty and repulsed by its destructive power. Here was power, totally divorced from man and money. It humbled him and made him feel afraid.

"We might as well go back," he told Rodriguez, pointing in the general direction of the lava flow. "Costanza's finished, anyway."

"Not yet," Rodriguez snapped. "Luis can always build another house, another zoo... if he's alive."

"The ground troops will be burned alive."

"I've already ordered them to turn around. We won't need them now."

The prospect of assaulting the Costanza rancho with a score of men—in spite of Mother Nature's grandiose diversion—tied Mercado's stomach into knots. He feared they wouldn't have a chance—especially now with every man on alert.

Rodriguez seemed to read Mercado's thoughts, a faint sneer on his lips. "Don't fret, José. They'll have their hands full, literally, saving everything they can carry from the fire."

And yet, as they approached the house, Costanza's people seemed to have their hands full with a different sort of problem. From a quarter mile Mercado picked out muzzle-flashes in the night and the sounds of explosions on the grounds.

There was a battle under way, and they were heading into it with twenty men.

"I thought you turned the others back."

"They had their orders," Rodriguez responded angrily. "Besides, they barely would have reached the place by now. This fighting's well along."

As if to prove his point, the east wing of the servants' quarters suddenly disintegrated, spewing shrapnel skyward on a tongue of flame.

There could be no mistake about the helicopter, though. He saw it clearly, rising from behind Costanza's mansion, sweeping to their left and hosing several antlike figures with a burst of automatic fire. A sudden pang of dark suspicion made him swivel toward Rodriguez, but his partner wore a blank, confused expression on his face.

"The DAS?" Mercado asked.

"They don't have anything like that."

"Who then?"

The gunship suddenly began to climb, as if the pilot had seen them coming. Moments later it was somewhere overhead and out of sight.

"You think we scared him off?"

"I don't know who *he* is," Mercado answered. "How am I supposed to tell you if the bastard's frightened?"

"You—"

He never got the comment out, since their companion airship suddenly began to veer and pitch like a demented animal, smoke pouring from the fuselage. Mercado twisted in his seat and saw another burst of gunfire rip through the cockpit, nailing both pilots to their seats.

A portion of Mercado's mind knew what was happening—the hostile gunship diving to attack—but shock prevented him from speaking as the wounded helicopter suddenly nosed over and dropped like a stone.

There was no need for shouted warnings, since their pilot had seen his comrades die. He instantly began evasive action, banking through a turn that pitched Mercado and Rodriguez against their safety harnesses. Mercado clutched his AK-47 in a death grip, knuckles bleached as white as bone, the weapon absolutely useless to him now.

Their helicopter was a military surplus transport model, used for hauling shipments of cocaine and sometimes—like tonight—delivering a hit team to selected targets. It wasn't a gunship, and the armor plating had been stripped away, since extra weight meant shorter range, and fuel took money.

They were helpless and effectively unarmed.

The pilot chose to run, his only option in the circumstances, cutting off the chopper's running lights and swinging back the way they'd come. The lava was his landmark, guiding him until he reached the mountains when the compass and altimeter would take control.

If they survived that long.

Mercado couldn't see the gunship on their tail, but it was closing all the same. One of the pilots gave a warning cry, and then a line of ragged holes marched across the left side of the fuselage, the bullets ripping into flesh when they had bored through steel. Blood splattered in Mercado's face as one of the hitters directly opposite his seat was nearly hacked in two.

The dealer felt his supper coming back and swallowed hard to keep it down, the effort wasted as a heavy bullet pierced his thigh and kept on going, through the pilot's seat to score a fatal hit. Mercado's scream was lost as something struck the engines and smoke began to fill the cabin.

Despite the tears and hacking cough, the agony below his waist, Mercado felt the chopper banking, going down. He caught a fleeting glimpse of fire below them, recognized the lava flow, and realized that they were plunging toward that crimson tide.

Rodriguez, buckled in the seat beside him, was a headless mannequin, blood soaking through his camouflage fatigues. Mercado cursed him, anyway, and in the moments left before they crashed, he just had time to scream.

MCPHERSON SPOTTED the gunners half a beat before Benning noticed them on the landing, and squeezed off a burst that dropped one where he stood and drove the other back. They must have had reserves, because at least two submachine guns instantly responded, firing blind along the stairwell, knocking divots out of the stucco wall.

McPherson saw his comrade reaching for a frag grenade and scuttled backward, crouched against the banister and made himself as small as possible. The blast was muffled, but it seemed to have a cataclysmic impact, sending mighty tremors through the house and rattling the stairs. A portion of the banister gave way behind McPherson, and he caught himself before the pull of gravity could suck him through the gaping hole.

"All clear!" Benning shouted.

McPherson started after him, but then another tremor rocked the house, much stronger than the last, accompanied by the sound of a tremendous blast.

"We're getting out of here," he ordered. "The whole thing's coming down."

Reluctantly the corporal doubled back and joined him in retreat, surrendering the shaky ground that they'd gained. McPherson told himself the hostages wouldn't have been upstairs in any case—or, if they were, Costanza would have whisked them out the moment he heard shooting on the grounds.

But if they *were* upstairs it was too late. A portion of the ceiling cracked above them and caved in, a broken timber ripping through the floor below. McPherson nearly lost his footing on the stairs, but saved it at the final instant, painfully rebounding off the nearest wall. Benning stumbled as they reached the ground floor, going down on one knee with an angry curse.

McPherson saw the big American approaching through a haze of plaster dust, Moore on his heels. There was no sign of the hostages, the dour expressions on their faces indicating defeat.

"Some kind of blast outside," he told McKay. "The house is cracking up. We've had it if we stay inside."

"Agreed. I have a feeling Costanza's slipped around us."

"He won't get far unless he's sprouted wings."

"My thoughts exactly," Bolan replied, already double-timing toward the nearest exit as he spoke.

McPherson fell in step behind him, the rest of the small team bringing up the rear and watching out for any surviving gunners who may have had the same idea. They reached the wide veranda unopposed, McPherson staring wordlessly at the spectacle of the eruption still in progress several miles away. The rivers of lava seemed much closer, but he couldn't calculate its speed.

"That tears it," the Mountie said. "How the hell are we supposed to find Costanza now?"

"You said yourself that he needs a pair of wings—or maybe rotors."

Flashing back to their review of bird's-eye photographs, McPherson grinned. "The airstrip or the heliport?"

"The chopper's closer. We can check it first."

"Right. Let's do it then."

The night had been transformed into a grim, surrealistic nightmare—gunfire and explosions, bodies scattered carelessly around the house, with the volcano spouting molten lava in the background. It was a touch of Dante modernized, but he had no time for a blow-by-blow critique.

They drew sporadic gunfire as they ran, returning it and dropping several of Costanza's soldiers on the grass.

The hand grenade came out of nowhere, bouncing several feet in front of Bolan. McPherson veered to his right and dived headlong toward the earth. A short fuse beat him to it, and the shock wave hit him like a fist, his body twisting in midair, lungs emptied as he landed on his back.

The Mountie thought he recognized Moore bending over him—or was it Benning? The stooping figure seemed to split apart, like an amoeba subdividing, then regained its solid shape before his eyes.

"You've got a problem there," McPherson said, and then the darkness carried him away.

KATZ EMPTIED his rifle's magazine, discarded it and snapped another into the receiver, rising from a crouch and moving past the two men he'd killed. They lay together, almost touching, dead eyes staring at a sky that had begun to fill with smoke and ash.

There was no sign of Manning or McCarter, but the servants' quarters were in flames, so they'd managed that all right. Katz didn't let himself consider whether they'd walked away, or not.

A zebra galloped past him in the darkness, followed closely by two more. Behind them, padding silently across the grass, a leopard seemed to have no interest in the zebras or the gray-haired man who kept him covered as he passed. Another moment and the cat was gone, a mottled shadow merging with the deeper shadows of the night.

Still following the great cat with his eyes, he missed the stationary gunner at his back, the first suggestion of a hostile presence striking Katz like a hammer stroke between the shoulder blades. The Kevlar vest saved his life, but he was facedown on the grass before he understood exactly what had happened, bruised and feeling starved for oxygen, a hellish ringing in his ears.

He knew enough to let the gunner think he was dead, his left hand lying open, precious inches from the holster on his hip. It was the worst position he could be in—awkward for a draw, his enemy behind him—but he had to play the cards as they were dealt. With any luck, if he lay still enough, the shooter might go in search of other targets, giving Katz his shot.

No luck.

His ringing ears picked up a muffled sound of footsteps on the grass, approaching at an angle, veering off a few yards short of contact. He was being circled now, the sniper checking him from different sides for signs of life.

Katz held his breath and kept his eyes wide open, trying for an out-of-focus look and praying he wouldn't blink involuntarily. One twitch would be enough to earn another bullet, and his enemy was close enough to put one through his head this time.

A pair of pointy cowboy boots appeared in front of him, with denim legs attached. The gunner kept his distance, and Katz was unable to be sure of anything above his waist. It was the wrong side for a draw, which required Katz to roll completely over as he pulled the automatic, roughly doubling his time and giving his opponent ample opportunity to fire a lethal burst.

Still, he'd have to try.

The rifle disappeared, now braced against the gunner's shoulder as he sighted for the coup de grace. Katz inched his left hand closer to his pistol, knowing in his heart he was out of time.

The gunner's scream was unexpected, mingled with a low, inhuman snarl. The boots and denim legs lurched out of range, and there was more snarling and another scream, accompanied by the sounds of scuffling on the grass.

Katz risked a peek in time to see a full-grown tiger rip the sniper's left arm from its socket, dropping it and bearing in with fang and claw to finish off its prey. Instinctively the Israeli scrambled to his feet, found his fallen rifle and backed off.

The tiger failed to notice—its jaws were locked around the sniper's face, and it snapped his neck with a convulsive twist, the rag doll figure going limp beneath its weight.

"Bon appétit," Katz whispered, and got the hell away from there.

Behind him, on the lawn, his benefactor settled down to feed.

GRIMALDI WATCHED the second chopper crash into the lava flow, a spout of flame erupting as the fuel tanks blew.

Concentrating on the task at hand, he doubled back to make another pass above the crumbling mansion and to look for friendly faces on the killing ground. The lava wasn't setting any land speed records, but it wasn't creeping, either. Bolan and his team were running out of time, no matter how you ran it down.

He spotted James and Encizo near the burned-out servants' quarters, trading fire with several of Costanza's gunners in the light of leaping flames. Grimaldi flanked the armed Colombians and came in on their blind side, skimming fifteen feet above the grass. He couldn't mask the sound of the rotors, but the 20 mm rounds from the Gatling guns got there ahead of any noise. The opposition scattered like a line of broken dummies underneath the hail of fire.

The LZ looked all right, but he made one more circuit of the field before he set the gunship down. Encizo was the first aboard, James close behind.

"The others?" the Stony Man pilot asked.

"Striker and the Mounties took the house," James said. "I'm hoping they were smart enough to give it back."

Costanza's mansion was a wreck, a portion of the roof collapsed, flames licking at the timbers underneath. There might be living men inside, but there was no way for Grimaldi to pick them out. "That still leaves three," he said, refusing to envision Bolan's body in the fire.

"Katz hit the stables," James told him. "Manning and McCarter went for the garage."

"Costanza and the hostages?"

The Phoenix warriors shook their heads.

"Okay, let's see who we can find."

THE FRAG GRENADE had gutted Benning and killed him where he stood. McPherson was unconscious, for the moment, and Moore had agreed to stay behind and keep him safe. Alone, the Executioner went looking for Costanza at the dealer's private helipad.

It could as easily have been the airstrip, with Costanza's Lear jet standing by, but he'd have to travel farther to the plane, and they'd decommissioned every rolling vehicle they could find. On foot the chopper was a decent bet, the airstrip elevated to a long shot with the stakes at life and death.

Abandoning the house had troubled Bolan, but he saw no choice. Costanza's instinct would be—*should* be—to preserve the hostages at any cost in case the battle turned against him. As it had, in fact. If he were driven into hiding, he'd still need chips to bargain with, perhaps for safe passage out of the country.

There was a chance, of course, that he'd left Dominga Franco and Andeana inside the house. A backward glance told Bolan there was nothing to be done in that event except to seek the fullest measure of revenge.

Scorched earth, accomplished with assistance from a creeping wall of fire.

They were emerging from a toolshed when he reached the heliport. Dominga and her daughter were in the lead, the implication obvious. Costanza had prepared himself against the seemingly impossible.

Survivors always thought ahead.

The chopper pilot had his engines warming up, but he hadn't engaged the rotors. Costanza cleared the shed before they started turning, lazily at first, then slowly picking up momentum.

Dominga and the child stopped short, intimidated by the whirling blades. Costanza prodded with his AK-47, urging them along.

From where he stood Bolan had a choice to make. One option was a simple shot to drop Costanza, but the dealer held his weapon at the ready, and a dying man could still squeeze off a lethal burst at point-blank range. Another was to challenge him and risk a confrontation, with the woman and her child as living shields. Costanza would likely back to the helicopter and drag them on board to make good his escape.

Which narrowed Bolan's range of choices to option number three.

He sighted quickly on the helicopter's windshield, found the pilot and fired a 3-round burst that took him out of play. Costanza reacted instantly, a wild blast from his AK-47 whipping over Bolan's head before the dealer ducked behind Dominga Franco, one arm looped around her neck. The child stood fast, terrified.

The right side of Costanza's head was frozen in Bolan's sights, but it would be a risky shot, the slightest deviation snuffing out Dominga's life, as well. Costanza could have fired one-handed, but he stopped himself, eyes wide and staring past his captive's head.

"Who are you?" he demanded, fear and anger mingled in his voice.

"I work for a collection agency," the Executioner replied. "We're calling in your note with interest due."

Costanza plainly didn't understand. "You're American?"

"That's right. Why don't you let the woman go, and we can settle this like men?"

"Like fools," Costanza spit. "I have another pilot for the helicopter. He's on his way."

It could have been the truth, but Bolan's adversary didn't sound convinced. "Trot him out. He won't be going far."

"The woman's life for mine," Costanza said. "The child I give you free of charge."

"No deals," he answered, conscious of the fact that his reply might make Costanza shoot the captives where they stood. "You're history."

"You spoke of debts. I pay mine off in different ways. Silver or lead. Your choice."

Dominga Franco made her move while Bolan's eyes were on Costanza and his weapon, but he caught the glint of metal in her fist, a slender shaft that pierced the dealer's cheek and burrowed deep, eliciting a howl of pain. The AK-47 stuttered as Dominga tore herself away and fell across her child, Costanza lurching backward, free hand rising toward the spike protruding from his face.

The magazine on Bolan's weapon emptied out in something like a second and a half, at least a dozen hits drilling Costanza before he toppled backward. A spreading pool of blood fanned out beneath him like the silhouette of broken wings.

Bolan knelt beside the prostrate woman and her child, Dominga flinching from his touch until she glanced up, vaguely recognizing his face.

"We're out of time," he said. "We have to go."

She nodded, and he helped them stand.

Feeling strong rotor wash at his back, the Executioner turned and saw the Cobra hovering, Grimaldi in the cockpit, grinning ear to ear. The Stony Man pilot's lips moved, and his voice was amplified from somewhere underneath the aircraft. "Somebody called a cab?"

He knew Grimaldi couldn't hear him, and he didn't even try to raise his voice as he replied, "You're right on time."

EPILOGUE

Scorched earth.

They didn't wait to see the flow of lava surge across Costanza's tennis courts, devouring his body on the helipad and finally encompassing the ruins of his grand palace. It was enough to know the job was done, and they had other stops to make—such as seeking medical attention for McPherson, Katz, James and Manning, and dropping off Dominga Franco and her daughter with a delegation of Sigfrido's comrades from the DAS, no questions asked.

The *federalistas* cheerfully informed Mack Bolan of the fact that Raul Rodriguez and José Mercado had departed for Costanza's rancho in a pair of helicopters earlier that evening. They hadn't returned, and it was Jack Grimaldi's pleasure to report they never would.

It was a wrap...but not an end.

The next morning Bolan and Grimaldi started north from Medellín by jeep and paid a visit to the rural church of Father Julio Lazaro. All things being equal, man and edifice alike had managed to survive the cataclysmic night. The sky was stained with soot but clearing, and the mountain that had spewed its guts the night before was simmering by daylight, easing back to sleep.

"I prayed for you," the priest said after they'd shaken hands.

"I know," Bolan told him.

"It was a sin perhaps, but God forgives an old man his mistakes."

"I wouldn't be surprised."

The Executioner was carrying a fat valise, which he gave to Lazaro, and smiled.

"A modest contribution to your parish."

"I'm tempted to inquire as to the source."

"We got it at the Lost and Found," Bolan replied. "Someone wandered off and left a safe-deposit box chock-full of money back in Medellín. The rumor is, he won't be needing it."

"Blood money," Lazaro said with a faint expression of distaste.

"I'd say that depends on how it's used. Maybe the only way to clean it up again is to turn around and put it to work for someone else."

The priest thought about that long and hard. His nod was visibly reluctant, but it came at last.

"You're leaving now?"

"We're finished here."

"For now."

"That's right. For now."

"I'm going soon myself."

Grimaldi flashed a smile. "And leave all this?"

"I won't be going far."

The warrior read his face and understood. "To better days," he said.

"God's will be done."

They left him standing in the churchyard, the valise in one hand, the other raised to wave goodbye.

"I don't know how he stood the place this long," Grimaldi said, a few miles down the unpaved, winding road.

"Because he loves it, Jack. Because it's home."

"That's it?"

"That's all it takes."

A HUNDRED MILES due east the pack train made its way along a narrow mountain track. The mules were laden with bundles wrapped in burlap sacking, with plastic underneath to keep the product fresh and pure. The point man for the train wore sandals made from rubber tires, a linen shirt and trousers in concession to the heat. He chewed a wad of coca leaf to pass the time.

It was another day, the morning giving way to afternoon, and he had a long way to go. At least fifteen miles remained before he met his contact in Barbosa and the deal was made. A lowly middleman, he wouldn't profit greatly from the trip, but it would feed his family and put clothes on their backs.

The rifle slung across his shoulder was heavy, a vintage piece from World War II, its polish long since faded to a satin sheen. So far the gun hadn't been necessary, and the peasant hoped his luck would hold.

You never knew these days, especially when men were dying left and right, shot down because they dabbled in cocaine and competed with the great cartels.

It was a risky trade, but he'd found his place and he was satisfied. A few more years of trekking through the mountains and he could retire instead of slaving in the coffee orchards until his back was stooped, his hair as white as the cocaine he carried from the jungle labs.

If he did well enough, perhaps he could afford a tidy house near Medellín, with land around it for a garden of his own. As long as he was loyal to his employer, duly cautious on the trail, he'd survive.

And he would prosper, in his way, as long as the gringos in the north loved to suck the powder up their noses or inject it into their veins.

It was a living, and the forest passed no judgment on his choice.

A few moments later the creeping train was lost to sight.

GOLD EAGLE

The Eagle now lands at different times at your retail outlet!

Be sure to look for your favorite action adventure from Gold Eagle on these dates each month.

Publication Month	In-Store Dates
May	April 24
June	May 22
July	June 19
August	July 24

We hope that this new schedule will be convenient for you.

Please note: There may be slight variations in on-sale dates in your area due to differences in shipping and handling.

GEDATES-R